FISH PIE and LAUGHTER

By

Eileen Dickson
Elaine Douglas
Vera Morris
Julie Roberts
Eve Wibberley

Chris + Faye - for fun!
I write as Eve (my middle
name + my maiden name)
Jennifer Eve

Jeeve Publishing

First published in Great Britain in 2005 by
Jeeve Publishing
PO Box 2696
Reading RG1 9BQ
Email: jeevepublishing@aol.com

ISBN 0 9550522 0 3
978 0 9550522 0 0

Third reprint, July 2009
Printed and bound in Great Britain by
Ridgeway Press, Ltd. Bramley, Hampshire

To our 'home alone' husbands!

We wish to thank:

Maureen Alan-Smith
Chris Mason, Ridgeway Press, Ltd
Reading Borough Council
Tony Roberts
Sue Tait
Jean Turner

Our chosen charity
Thames Valley and Chiltern Air Ambulance Trust

Contents

AUGUST
The Swanwick Babes

The car drew up in front of The Chequers. They smiled at each other; the magic was holding. The week the five friends had been together in Derbyshire had been perfect August weather. In Cornwall, cars had been washed out to sea, houses wrecked and cream had curdled. In Scotland, roads had been engulfed by mudslides, bridges collapsed and bagpipes had bloated and burst. They had had tea on the lawn, cocktails on the terrace and a week of sheer enchantment and stimulation with two hundred and sixty other writers.

The journey from Derbyshire to Oxfordshire had been smooth and fast, the weather sunny, but as they stood outside the pub they noted a large black cloud on the horizon. They looked at each other. Would the bubble burst? Could the return to reality be approaching?

Fish Pie and Laughter

Settling into the conservatory of the pub, they arranged themselves at one of the four round tables that were covered in cloths featuring fruit and flowers. It was a cosy room with a grape vine decorating the glass roof, red walls, a terracotta tiled floor. There was a view of the small garden: an old apple tree, some bench seats, a bird bath supported by a disconsolate putto.

They studied the blackboard menu.

'I'll have prawn cocktail,' said Julie.

'I think the cauliflower cheese for me,' Eve said.

'That sounds nice, I'll have the same,' said Elaine.

'Oh, fish pie, I love fish pie!' Vera smiled in anticipation.

'So do I. Make that two,' agreed Eileen.

Drinks ordered, they once more settled round the table.

'You happy there?' the barmaid asked. 'Only the roof's a bit leaky and it looks as though we're in for a storm.'

'We're fine,' they chorused. They were protected by their Swanwick bubble. What could happen to them?

There was a flash of lightning and the sky flung its contents at the roof of the conservatory. All conversation ceased as they watched a small river gurgle its way across the floor towards them, veer to the right and disappear under the wall into the garden. There were shrugs and smiles; they didn't care. They were certainly not water babies, or even nymphs, they were the Swanwick babes.

Vera

SEPTEMBER
Of bras, canoes and Labradors

They were so keen to meet, to exchange stories and ideas, they arrived at The Chequers before it opened at mid-day. They milled around outside, admiring the hanging baskets, possibly being viewed by passers-by as desperate lushes in search of drink.

Safely seated in the conservatory, the conversation veered between reasons for needing time of one's own for writing, to the exploration of Reading's subterranean water world. Next month, they decided, they would have a theme.

Summer School

It had been Ginny who persuaded her to join the Creative Writing Group.

'Honestly, Liz, you'll love it. There's only a bit of homework to do each week, and we go to the pub afterwards. Better than housework any day. And David Miles is a dish.'
Liz had not considered paunchy David Miles to be a dish, but then she was spoiled with James. And it would stretch her own small world which had been so bound up with his and, until latterly, the children. And so she had gone.

'Are you sure you don't think I should get a job, James?' she'd asked one evening over their ritual gin and tonic.

A strand of fair hair had fallen across her face, and her blue eyes looked directly into his.

'*You*, my darling, already have a job and that's me – *I'm* very demanding and you're very good at it. Besides, what else could you do?' He stopped, seeing her face and put his arms around her. 'Darling Lizzie, forgive me, you know I didn't mean it – we'd all collapse without you.'

'It's just,' she said, fighting to find the right words, 'it's just that I don't do very much except be here for you and the garden and the children, but now that they're away...' She looked up at him to see if he understood.

James smiled gently at her. 'You're quite right, my love, and whatever you decide to do will have my blessing. As long as you're here when I want you then you can do anything you like.'

Later, the idea of going to the Writers' Summer School seemed a natural consequence.

'You've simply got to come with us, Liz,' said Rose earnestly. 'I went last year, and it's great fun. Just think, no cooking, cleaning – or husbands,' she added darkly, 'and lots of interesting people all talking about writing.'

Elizabeth thought the last bit sounded rather exhausting but was too polite to say so.

'*And,*' Ginny added enthusiastically, 'we get to meet real publishers who tell you what they want you to write about so you're ahead of the game.'

'Has it helped you get anything published?' Elizabeth asked.

Ginny shot her a cross look. If it had been anyone other than dear Lizzie she might have suspected sarcasm. 'Well, not yet, but at least I know what they *don't* want. Anyway, they'll remember me when they get the script.'

'Well, that's good,' said Elizabeth comfortingly.

And, as they both wanted it so much, she had gone.

Eileen

Mad, Mad Husband

Who in their right mind, would canoe under the town of Reading? Well, my husband, Tony, and his canoe partner, Bob, did just that!

They were practising for the 125-mile Easter weekend Devizes to Westminster Canoe Race. It is an annual event that uses the Kennet and Avon Canal, the River Thames and the tidal reach from Teddington.

One Sunday morning they had planned a practice run down the Thames.

Imagine - a narrow twenty-two foot long canoe called a K2, with two young men leaning into their strokes skimming downstream from Caversham Lock. A decision to change course into the Kennet Canal, portage Blakes Lock, then take the Abbey backwater alongside Reading Prison.

Why deviate, you wonder? Might practising get a bit boring? Perhaps they wanted a change of scenery?

At the west-end of the backwater, the Holybrook emerges. This is the stream that used to bring water to Reading Abbey.

Curiosity led them *upstream* into the brook, until they came to a tunnel, about ten feet wide and high enough to enter.

Only mad-cap youth would dare venture inside.

They didn't even have a torch.

Picture their journey:

Light fading from behind, darkness ahead. Only the sound of running water and the dip of paddles. Feel the air chill and touch the wet walls. Hear the scratching of rats and wonder what creepy-crawly is running over your damp back. Blackness, that blots out everything. Just disembodied voices, echoing words.

Paddle under the Kings Road junction.

Dim light from a barred drain, like a prison window.
Under the 200-year-old cobbled courtyard of the George Hotel.
Ahead, a circle of daylight.
Out into the open.
Paddle past the hotel kitchen window and a surprised chef.
Back into a tunnel.
Dipping those paddles under the Post Office Telephone Exchange, then into daylight at Minster Street.
The Holybrook swings left and goes underground again.
Snakes under Simonds Brewery in Bridge Street. Under its great beer vats and cobbled yard.
On under Fobney Street. Past County Lock.
Continual blackness broken only by the occasional drain-grille, or badly-fitting manhole cover.
Then, after an adventure of no more than a mile, out into sunlight at Brook Street.
Journey's end.

I'm sure, it was at this point, they questioned the recklessness of what they had done. Thoughts such as: how do you turn a twenty-two foot canoe in a ten foot wide tunnel or get unstuck when the roof lowered and they had to use their shoulders? Youth the explorer, rarely considers such things. And the sight of a racing canoe being carried, at a run, through Reading on a Sunday morning in 1974 was less of an oddity then than it might be today.

My reaction when they arrived home? 'Oh. You paddled under Reading? How nice. Lunch is nearly ready.'

Julie

Arrested

'Who were the publicans at the Bottle and Glass? I remember one of them was disabled. It's a lovely old pub,' reminisced Eve.

'You must be thinking of Harry and Rene,' replied Vera. 'It was Rene who was crippled; she had numerous operations on her hips and knees, but she had a wonderful spirit, quite indomitable. Trevor and I knew them very well.

'I must tell you a story; it involves Harry and our two dogs. We were regulars at the Bottle and Glass, enjoying the roaring log fires, the real ale and the great craic. Harry and Rene had two males from a litter of Labradors and persuaded us that their two sisters needed a good home. There were many bonds between us.

'I'll always remember the night Harry spent sleeping downstairs, with the door open, in case our two dogs, Holly and Jet, who'd absconded, made their way back there. It wasn't the first time they had gone missing; they were rabid hunters and, once on the scent, wouldn't be diverted. Some months earlier, they had disappeared from Clayfield Copse on a snowy winter's night. It was quite late when Harry rang to say the two dogs were at the pub. Jet was chasing the cats and Holly was eating the cats' food.

'This night they had gone missing in the woods near the pub. Searching and shouting brought no results. Harry moved a camp bed down to the main bar, saying he would phone us if they came back. Luckily it wasn't a winter's night, it was May, but we were grateful for his vigil. Trevor and I spent a sleepless night, imagining all sorts of nightmare scenarios. At five o'clock I asked Trevor to phone Henley Police Station, to see if they had been involved in an accident.'

'Two dogs? Look like Labradors?'

Oh no! 'Yes, what has happened?'

'They were brought in yesterday evening, found near Rotherfield Greys. Chap saw them in a field, called, they went into his car, no trouble. They're in the dog cells.'

'Have they collars on? Can you read their tags?'

'Too dangerous to approach. I think they've got collars on.'

'I'll be right over.'

'There will be a fine, sir. Night's board, care and attention.'

We were so overjoyed that we didn't bother to point out how friendly they were, and that a phone call from the police the previous evening would have eased our hearts. It would also have prevented the convicts having empty stomachs, a serious condition in a dog, especially a Labrador, and Harry could have rested comfortably in his proper bed.

The reunion was fantastic and we all met at the Bottle and Glass to toast the return of Holly and Jet. The dogs were firmly tethered by their leads.'

Vera

8

Daddy's Drowning –
Let's have an Ice Cream

A fortnight in Hope Cove staying in the boss's holiday home – such luxury. But not only the house, a little sailing dinghy too! What fun we were going to have with our three small children and Edward, the fifteen-year-old 'au pair' boy, my widowed sister's son who earned his nickname over several holidays spent with us.

On a sunny afternoon, James and Edward set off to try out the dinghy, leaving me with our three, aged eight downwards, on the beach. Closely watched by the families on the sands, off they bravely sailed. All went well for some time. There was sufficient wind to fill the sail and the little vessel danced over the waves as they tacked across the bay. Whilst I helped build castles, dispense drinks, remove sand from eyes and collect various paraphernalia from the water, I glanced from time to time at the progress on the high seas.

Suddenly there was an 'Aaaah!' from everyone around. Startled, I looked up to see the dinghy had capsized and two small figures were floundering in the water. The people on the beach stood up to watch proceedings, muttering urgently amongst themselves. Feeling sick but trying to hide this from our children, I said cheerfully, 'Come on, let's go and find some ice cream.' As we left the beach, I was aware of some curious looks from the sunbathers closest to us, who were probably horrified at my apparent lack of concern for those in peril on the sea, particularly as they'd doubtless guessed the figures struggling in the water were related to us.

Arms flailing and heads bobbing, James and Edward were taking ages to right the boat. We walked around licking our ice creams as I chatted aimlessly about anything that came into my head. The children were very quiet and looked at me strangely. Maybe they were wondering whether they'd ever see their Daddy or cousin again.

Eventually, an old boatman, mumbling what sounded like 'too lumpy for Jeffrey,' rowed to the rescue. Edward was blue and shivering. What would his mother say if she could see her precious son now? James had refused to allow him to try and swim ashore – hence the row – and the boat had proved too cumbersome to haul upright because its dagger board was lost beneath the waves.

To this day the sea is always 'too lumpy for Jeffrey' whenever it's a little rough. A reminder that 'Daddy's drowning - let's have an ice cream'.

Eve

Bother in Budapest

My recent visit to Budapest was packed with interesting happenings but one little incident has me bewildered. Michael and I stay in our son's small elegant third-floor apartment, which has two balconies, one outside our bedroom and the other outside the sitting room, both containing boxes and tubs of plants. I am in the habit of rinsing out small items of clothing early each morning and hanging them over a wire contraption placed in the corner of the balcony outside the bedroom.

A few days before we were due to return to England the weather changed and, instead of mild sunny days, we had gusty winds and rain. Without thinking, I performed my usual routine and, on returning to the balcony with my second bowl of socks and underpants, I realised that although the two bras were hanging there, one pair of panties was missing. Fallen onto the floor – no – could they have blown through one of the gaps or over the top of the balustrade and got caught on a branch or dropped onto the balcony below?

Peering down into the street, there they were, a forlorn blob on the pavement. There was no one around. I decided to go down and retrieve my garment, although I'd probably put it in the rubbish bin. Grabbing a cardigan to put over my head as it was now raining, I left the flat, went down in the lift, through the entrance once used for horses and carriages, out through the massive door into the street where there were a few passers-by, ran round the corner to where I had seen the offending article – nothing. I looked up. Yes, here was the place. I checked and double checked, wandered about, looking up at our balcony every now and again. Conscious that other occupants of the street were looking at me strangely, I decided to give up my search.

What had happened to the missing panties with a front panel of lace? Were they in the gutter covered by leaves, or had one of the many homeless with their sharp eyes, foraging around, discovered my runaway embarrassment? I'll never know but will certainly buy some clothes pegs to use next time I visit.

Elaine

OCTOBER
Not fish pie again!

It was the last day of October, the sky was overcast and though it was only mid-day, the lantern wall lights were glowing brightly in the conservatory as the five women decided what to eat.

'You're not having fish pie again, Vera?' Eileen rolled her eyes, 'Do you eat nothing but fish pie?'

'I like fish pie. If you let me have fish pie, I'll tell you a ghost story.'

'As long as it isn't about an ethereal haddock,' joked Julie.

'Or the spirit of a sprat,' said Eve.

With great dignity, Vera replied, 'No, this has nothing to do with fish.'

Masterstroke

'Hiya, Jimmy, see you've got the easy shift tonight.' Gareth's black face creased into a smile.

'I can't tell you how glad I am to get away from that exhibition; load of modern rubbish. You should have heard the punters, drooling over elephant dung and obscene mannequins.'

'You didn't like that pickled shark then?'

James Locke shook his bald head fringed with white merino fluff, matching his beard. 'That Mr. Saatchi, calls himself an art lover…'

'You'll be all right with this lot then. It's been crowded today. Can't understand it myself, all this interest in fairies.'

The lighting was low in the Sackler wing of the Royal Academy of Arts. James gazed around at the paintings in

Room One - Victorian Fairy Paintings. He nodded approvingly. Bit weird, but at least they weren't rude.

'Hey, Jimmy, before I forget, look in Room Two, the Dadd picture, one on the far right; there's a guy in that painting, he's the spitting image of you.' He handed over the pager and, whistling cheerily, left the room.

James sat on one of the mahogany benches and pulled out food from his back pack. Making sure he didn't leave any crumbs, he nibbled his way through a cheese sandwich. He'd been pleased to be asked to stand in for a security man who'd been taken ill; he didn't mind a night shift, no-one to go home to.

He wandered around; in Room Two he looked for the picture Gareth had mentioned. First he read about the artist, Richard Dadd, from the details on the wall: 'The greatest Victorian Fairy Painter was Richard Dadd (1817-1886)...' his eyes skimmed over the details until, 'in 1843 Dadd murdered his father and was confined in Bethlam Hospital lunatic asylum, later being transferred to Broadmoor.' He turned away, not wanting to read further. He felt sick. He must have eaten that sandwich too fast.

He looked at Dadd's paintings; wonderful technique. The fifth painting, the one Gareth had mentioned, was titled *The Fairy Feller's Masterstroke.* James felt as though he was lying on the ground, peering through the tall grasses painted in the foreground. In the centre, the Fairy Feller, his back to James, double-headed axe raised above his head, aimed at a hazel nut on the ground. Around him were many figures: Titania and Oberon, dwarves, magicians, tinker, tailor, soldier, sailor and, to his right, a handsome young man, black hair falling from a high forehead, staring intently at the axe man. In front of the Fairy Feller, squatting on the ground, his hands on his knees, a look of terror in his eyes was himself: the bald head, the white beard, the straight nose. James felt a roaring in his ears. Swaying, he staggered to a central bench, gulping for air. He thrust his head between his knees; gradually the feeling of panic faded.

He felt a tug at his sleeve. A young man, seated besides him, smiled.

'Sorry, sir, I didn't feel too well. Are you from the office? Were you trying to get me on the pager?' James said. The young man shook his head, his dark hair, falling across his face. 'I don't know you, sir. Are you new to the Academy?'

The young man laughed. 'I have often been a visitor and indeed an exhibitor. I have been waiting to meet you for a long time.'

James was sure he knew him, he'd seen that face before. The young man was foppishly well-dressed: a shirt with a high starched collar, a waistcoat and a tightly-fitting jacket which flared at the waist.

'You've waited for me, sir? I don't understand.'

'We are the same. I understand you.' He raised his right hand and five icicles caressed James's cheek. 'I know why you had to do it. It was the same for me. He would not leave her alone. Each night I would hear her screams, her pleadings, but he would not stop. Each year another child, until she was dead. He was Satan, he had to die. They caught me, brought me back from France, to live the rest of my life amongst mad people.'

'Who... who are you? Why are you telling me this?' The cold was creeping down from his cheek to his throat and chest, squeezing the air from his lungs.

'You have been lucky; you were never suspected. Only I share your secret, whilst the world shares mine.' The young man pulled James to his feet and dragged him towards the picture.

'Come, we will join my friends. We will eat hazel nuts and listen to Titania tell a story.' James tried to resist, to reach his pager, but his arms were frozen to his sides. The young man pointed to the painting. 'See, the Fairy Feller and all his friends are waiting.'

The figures in the painting, all as tall as the young man, were moving. James could hear the wind blowing through the grasses, smell the dank, mossy wood. The long trumpet and the French horn blared their sounds through the night air, Titania inclined her crowned head and Oberon saluted him with his feathered staff. There was a white space to the right of the axe man. James looked round at the young man, who stepped back into the picture.

The Fairy Feller lowered his axe, turned and stepped out of the frame. James collapsed to the floor, eyes tightly shut.

'Look at me, James, I command you,' said a deep voice. Slowly he opened his eyes. He saw feet encased in black boots, strong gaitered legs, wide shoulders covered in a leather coat, a face in shadows, a woollen cap partially covering dark, straight hair.

The Fairy Feller raised his axe and James saw his face.

'Father!' he screamed and his chest exploded with pain.

They found him at the end of the shift. He was crumpled in front of the picture, knees pulled up to his chest, eyes staring in horror.

The doctor, confirming death, thought the dead man had had a massive stroke. Noting the right hand, clenched in a tight fist, he prised open the cold fingers; a small hard object fell from James's palm and rolled across the floor; it was a hazelnut.

Vera

Bird in a Gilded Cage

The Encounters Exhibition at the Victoria and Albert Museum was packed with people on the last day in November 2004, making it almost impossible to get a good look or to appreciate the things on display. However, our daughter, having visited the exhibition before, guided Michael and I around and we bought some postcards in the shop before leaving, which I pushed into a drawer at home.

Christmas came and went with the usual bustle, shopping, decorating, opening mail from far and wide and, just as welcome, from around the corner. Guests arrived and we went to church, enjoyed walks, meals, conversation and then came the devastating news of the Tsunami Disaster, which put life into perspective for everyone around the globe. After First Footing our guests departed.

Looking through a drawer, I came across the cards from the V&A and was drawn to one, a picture of the Imperial Concubine of Emperor Yonzheng at the Qing Court of China (1723-35) from the Collection of the Palace Museum, Beijing.

Gazing out of her apartment window, this beautiful young woman sits serene and languid at her intricately carved desk, writing implements ready for use, a hand-painted scroll on the wall behind her. Two kittens play mischievously around her tightly bound feet. Her stiffly coifed black hair is held in place by jade combs. The delicate painted features of her white oval face appear wistful, if not sad. In the background an attendant kneels sorting out combs and jewellery into exquisite boxes, whilst her horologist kneels at a small table consulting her charts.

What attracts this pampered woman's attention to the garden? Is it laughter and chatter from the cook's children, helping pick peaches and carefully laying them in a shallow basket? Others are darting in and out of the shrubs whilst an older girl picks lotus blossom for another basket. These little children, brightly clad, are happy and carefree, just like the birds in the enclosed garden,. Who knows what they will do, where they will go? Whilst she, brought to Court as a child, has her life mapped out before her. Her destiny is written in the charts, her every whim and desire attended to but, like a bird of paradise, she will be kept forever in a gilded cage.

Today many of us have opportunities and freedom beyond our wildest dreams. The young Concubine of the Chinese Court could never have envisaged the emancipation science has given to the world's population of the 21ˢᵗ Century, especially to women. However, we are still unable to prevent the disaster caused by a tsunami.

Elaine

Another Mary Celeste?

Tony, Mark and John were looking forward to a wife-less weekend sailing. Maybe they'd end up in Lymington and enjoy a meal in the little restaurant below the laundry. Last time the owner had plied them with eggs and bacon to take back for their breakfast; doubtless she'd heard enough of their chat-up lines and wanted to close for the night.

John would drive down to Portsmouth in the afternoon to bring his Westerly, *Mirabelle,* from its swing mooring back to the jetty and meet Tony and Mark in the pub at about seven o'clock. On his way, John would collect a second-hand outboard. He unloaded and inflated the dinghy, mounted the motor and set out across the harbour. After a hundred yards the engine died. He pulled repeatedly on the cord and almost fell overboard when it broke. The oars were on *Mirabelle.* Undaunted, he took up one of the dinghy's floorboards and, in the gathering gloom, paddled crab-wise to a moored yacht showing its mast light. He shouted and shouted but there was no reply. Climbing gingerly aboard, he felt unnerved by the silence. All the hatches were open and, peering into the lighted cabin, he could see the remains of a meal on the table – definitely past its sell-by date from the smell! It was obvious there had been a hasty departure.

Back on deck, John noticed a Royal Navy patrol vessel not far away. He attracted attention by yelling and leaping about waving his arms. They came to his rescue but were as mystified as he as to the whereabouts of the owners of this *Mary Celeste,* swinging gently on her mooring.

The patrol boat sped John and his dinghy to *Mirabelle.* At last, all he had to do was start the engine, move the vessel across to the jetty and collect his mates. No such luck. The batteries were flat, but he had a starting handle. In the dark and in his eagerness, he bent it. Oh well, he did now have the oars. Replacing the floorboard in the dinghy and sitting on a petrol can, he rowed the mile back to shore in the dark.

As he staggered into the Jolly Roger some three hours late, tired, wet and exhausted, Tony looked up from his beer and declared 'It's your round!'

The mystery of the *Mary Celeste* has never been fathomed.

Eve

Ask the Gremlins

'Have you seen my keys?'
　'No.'
　'They were here yesterday.'
　'Which keys?'
　'Door keys.'
　'No.'
　'I've looked everywhere. Are you sure?'
　'Yes.'
　'Have a look for me.'
　'No.'
　'Why not. I'm late. Can I have yours?'
　'No.'
　'Will you be here when I get back?'
　'No.'
　Drawers open and shut. Cupboard doors bang.
　It's a repeat performance every time.
　Wait for it – here it comes - another set of keys to be cut?
　'Lend me yours, I'll pop down the shop to get a new set.'
　'Another fiver less for the savings fund.'
　'Look on the bright side, a spare set when we find them.'

Three months later.
　'Pass my Wellingtons. Best take them on holiday, then it
won't rain.'
　'What's that rattling inside the left boot?'
　'A set of door keys.'
　'How did they get there?'
　'I don't know. Ask the gremlins.'

Julie

Consequences

'I won't be long love. Anyway, Mum'll chuck me out a'fore nine so's she can watch *Frost*.'

Tom laughed; he knew his mother well and thought for the thousandth time what a saint Mary was, trotting along to see the old girl who had a tongue like a razor..

'And we'll have the cold lamb and new potatoes for supper when I get back,' Mary said.

'That'll be grand. Now don't let her scold you, she's no call to do that when you're so good to her.' (And rather you than me, he added, under his breath.)

'Oh, she don't mean it, Tom, does her good to have the odd moan. I don't listen most of the time. Anyway, at her age you run out of people you can be nasty to without them taking offence. There's some cold rice pudding you could have with a bit of cream if you're peckish,' she said, fastening her sturdy sandals in the hall.

'Be off, woman, or you'll not be back before midnight, then *I'll* get nasty!'

They both smiled at the ludicrous thought, and he watched her affectionately as she dropped a tin of peaches and some chocolate digestives along with her mother-in-law's washing into her shopping bag. Anyway, he reassured himself, it wasn't far along the road from their bungalow to the cottage outside the village.

'Be a good chap and pop another one in there will you?' Giles Crawshaw had had a really good day. The property market showed no sign of slowing down and he'd virtually clinched the deal on that tasty bit of land the other side of Speen. Gerry had said the old chap was almost ripe for selling, couldn't last out much longer.

The Hungry Magpie was full for a Thursday, and Molly, the landlady, didn't stop to have her usual little flirt with him. She emerged from the other bar with a tray full of drinks for the upstairs meeting room.

'Bloody Masons,' she said, 'all that secret handshaking doesn't stop their drinking arms,' and she disappeared up the stairs with the slopping tray.

'Sorry to keep you waiting, Giles, you can see how it is tonight.' Bill Johnson was apologetic, not wanting to offend one of his best customers.

'No worries, Bill, but better make that a double to save time - oh, and whatever you're having yourself.'

A couple of large Jamiesons later, Giles emerged from the pub. He couldn't quite remember where he'd left the Jag. It took him a couple of minutes to locate it and fit the key into the lock, but he was smiling to himself as he pulled out on to the Newbury Road. Bloody good day all round. Penny had better watch out for herself tonight, p'raps he could get her to wear that black lacey thing he'd bought her at Christmas and she'd never worn. Funny that, she went to all those aerobic thingeys at the health club to keep her body up to scratch, yet she was always tired when he...

The heavy car veered up on to the verge and hit something.

'Bloody hell, that wasn't there last time.' Giles swore and tried to make out through bleary eyes what he'd hit. Fox, probably. Better not have damaged the paintwork. Scotts charged through the nose for the smallest job. Still, once this deal was done he'd not have to worry about little garage people.

Sitting on the wooden garden bench, Tom finished his pipe and looked with satisfaction over the freshly dug patch where he'd planted beans and potatoes earlier that day. He liked listening to the evening sounds and smelling the young spring earth. An owl hooted in Netherton Woods and he thought he might just go and have a spoon of that rice pudding. Mary must be due back soon.

Newbury Police Station was quiet that evening, and, as luck would have it, Tom's old friend, John Bryce, was on the Front Desk when he came in. The two men had been boys together at Sheep Common Primary School a long time back, and had broken most of the known rules there without discovery.

'Tom! How you doing? Long time no see.'

'John, I'm glad it's you. Listen, I feel a bit silly, but it's Mary. She hasn't come home.' He was relieved the policeman didn't make a pat response. 'She went to see my Mum and she hasn't come back. I phoned Mum, but she said Mary had left.'

'I'm sure there's a simple explanation, Tom, but leave it with me. You go back to the house now. You'll most like find she's there and you'll get a roasting for being out with loose women from Newbury Town.'

'An' you'll know them all, John, no doubt.' With difficulty, Tom managed a smile but recognised the sense of the suggestion.

John Bryce liked police work. He liked the sense and the regularity of it, but most of all he liked the working out of things. Most people followed a pattern. All you had to do was to work out the patterns and you were there.

He started very slowly at one end of Mary's walk and proceeded to the end. He was not surprised to find a sandal in the hedge where hawthorn budded and cuckoo-pint and burdock were coming into flower. And further back from where the body had been hit, a plastic shopping bag lay in the grass.

The next morning, he went to the pub and on to the garage and talked to people he'd known for most of his life.

'God, Giles, what a ghastly thing?' Penny came into the kitchen holding the local newspaper. 'Some bastard did a hit-and-run on the Newbury Road Thursday night and poor Mary Whatsit's been killed. You remember her, Giles, she used to clean for us.'

Giles did not remember. He had a splitting headache, but dimly recalled the thud on the car. Christ, must make sure the car's OK. More importantly, his mind now racing, must make sure that *he* was.

'Penny, darling, I do rather think we deserve a little holiday and I need to look at that Spanish property I bought outside Seville last year - maybe the right time for a spot of development?'

At the inquest the death was recorded as 'Death by Driver or Drivers Unknown' and became a statistic.

Several months later, a Spanish police car drew up outside Casa Verde and presented the owner, Mr Giles Crawshaw, with an extradition warrant to return to England in connection with manslaughter charges against him.

In Sheep Common, the beans needed picking and the potatoes needed digging, but Tom didn't see much point any more.

Eileen

NOVEMBER
The Dead Worm

The vine had lost its leaves and rain drizzled from a dark grey sky. Behind Eve's chair, a desiccated earthworm lay coiled in a mysterious knot on the tiled floor. They studied the pattern of death intently, as if it might augur approval of their stories, stories of their brushes with authority.

Brush with the Law

Summer 1975

It was Sunday and there was very little traffic on the roads. The police van with two armed policemen, one driving, the other beside him with walkie talkie, made its way from Sea Point, a popular seaside residential area with many restaurants and art galleries, into and through Cape Town, up the hill through Newlands and Bergvliet and on into the wooded region of Tokai. This journey took about half-an-hour. The other occupants of the police van were two adults in their early forties, casually dressed in summer clothes. They were seated in the back of the vehicle and behind the grille in the back portion of the van were three children, blond, tanned, healthy; a boy about seven, girl nine and a toddler, also a girl, plus two large Alsatian guard dogs. The midday sun shone in through the windows making it uncomfortably hot in the rear of the van but, at last, the driver pulled into a quiet close and turned the engine off.

Having got out and walked to the back of the van, the policemen unlocked the door and the children and dogs spilled out onto the hot tarmac, chattering happily and patting the dogs. Meanwhile the couple got out and joined children, dogs and policemen at the gate to the garden and house in front of them. Neighbours in gardens or on their steps gazed at the group in consternation. What was going on? Why were the police and dogs escorting this family into their home? In South Africa decent good living church-going folk did not get involved with the law. None of the onlookers came out to greet their neighbours. No one called out; no one came to their aid - silence - until the little boy called out:

'Isn't it great, we came home with the police in their van! Daddy couldn't get the car to start after we went to the beach. Wait till I tell everyone at school!'

We were the family who caused the stir one sunny Sunday afternoon in a leafy suburb of Cape Town. But what would have happened had we really been in trouble?

Elaine

The Big Squeeze

At six foot six and heavily built, Ken was too large to fit into the police cell. Neither he nor James spoke sufficient Arabic to make the officer understand that James was in no position to sign a surety guaranteeing his boss would remain in the Sudan for the court case.

It had not been a good week and, as agent on the contract building Berth 15, the buck stopped at Ken.

It all began last:

Sunday

As a five-ton block was being lifted, the crane jib folded. Another crane trundled through town from the main quay. Its jib clipped the flimsy telephone wires at the dock entrance, cutting off the guard's communication. Sabotage! The crane driver was arrested. Ken negotiated all morning before the crane driver was allowed to return to work.

In the afternoon of that hot July day, the crane was returning to the main quay and the banksman, who should have been walking ahead, took a ride. Sadly, he fell off and was killed, so the crane driver was arrested for the second time. Then it transpired he had no driving licence.

Monday

The damaged crane had to go to the workshop. However, on checking, it was discovered its driver had no licence either. The only person with a driving licence was the chief fitter, who couldn't drive cranes. So the driver stood behind the fitter in the cab and instructed him which lever to push or pull as they made their way through town.

Tuesday

The UK foreman and the store man hadn't turned up for work. Where were they? They hadn't been back to the Mess the previous night. Ken found them in gaol. Monday evening, they had been entertaining some British sailors and were the worse for drink when they drove their visitors back to the ship, not bothering to stop at the customs post. The officials caught up with them as they were loading cigarettes and beer into their pick-up. The sailors were brought before the court in the morning and given a six weeks' prison sentence. Ken had to go to their ship to advise the captain and pay bail for his own men.

Thursday

The police asked Ken to come with them to the station. James followed him as a precaution and then the problem arose - how to squeeze Ken into a prison cell. There was no way he could even get through the door. Finally, James signed the surety for a hundred pounds, which was more than he could spare in 1960.

Eve

This Way, Please

In a convoy of two and a half, we were driving along the M4 towards the Severn Bridge. The wind blew a near hurricane and the rain was coming down like stair-rods.

Ahead of me, soaked to the skin, Tony was riding his 1961 Norton motorbike.

The 'half' was the trailer behind my car, towing Horace, a 1934 Royal Enfield. What a night to have come out. I should have waited until morning. But it was too late for 'if only' thoughts.

The one not vexed was the circular cushion of ginger and white fur curled on the passenger seat. From time to time his paw twitched - probably dreaming of mice.

Out of the darkness a warning sign flashed: the bridge was closed to high-sided vehicles and caravans.

This wasn't for me. My little trailer didn't come under this order.

As the miles decreased, the warning signs appeared again.

Not for me, mate. I'm going across the bridge.

What's that up ahead? It looks like a queue of traffic. I don't need this. I'm tired and this awful weather is straining my eyes.

There's a policeman waving a torch. Why? He's turning the lorries and caravans off down the slip road just before the bridge. That means they have to go the long way round, up to Gloucester.

Hell's bells!

What's he doing, waving me off! I've only got a little motorbike on the back.

OK, OK.

Let's pretend.

If you think I'm going via Timbuktu, you have another thought coming. There's plenty of room between the cones for my little car to get back through!

What's wrong with this? I'm crossing the bridge fine.

I wonder where Tony is? I haven't seen him for ages. He disappeared into the darkness miles back.

I hope he's waiting for me on the other side, I don't know the way to Whitecroft. I don't have a map.

You want to know what happened?

Knowing that trailers were being turned off, he was waiting for me down at the roundabout below the bridge. Then saw me go driving across.

I won't print what he was calling me. Just to say, he crossed the bridge on the cyclists' path!

Abandoned, I drove purely from what I had seen on the map days before. And we both arrived at the campsite within ten minutes of each other.

How's that for dead reckoning navigation?

Julie

The Scrump

My sister was the undisputed Leader of our Gang. She swaggered about with her snake-clasp belt hung with penknives and wore shorts whenever she could. Pat was fierce because she'd wanted to be a boy and that's how boys were. The other member was Tommy Gasson, the cowman's son. His mother had wanted a girl, so she dressed Tommy in baby girl dresses till he was about four, when Mr Gasson finally got his way and Tommy 'came out' in boys' clothes. Tommy always liked playing with our dolls. Mrs Gasson had a fetish about cleanliness, and rag rugs overlaid with newspaper covered the floors in their cottage. We felt sorry for Tommy. Sometimes Susan Brittlehawke from Bottom Farm was allowed to be in the Gang but my sister bossed her about so she didn't come very often.

'We don't want her, she can't take orders,' Pat pronounced at the last Gang meeting.

And I was the last member, tolerated only because of my age and my usefulness for running errands.

In 1948, Pat was nine and I was seven. We lived in the grounds of a preparatory school and my mother was housekeeper to a schoolmaster called Mr Box. We had the run of the school estate, with its fat, grass-fed ponies, limitless woods and fields. In summer we rarely came home before dark. There weren't many other children around; a few from the big houses, some from the farms and us.

One summer morning in the school holidays, we decided to raid the Fanshawes' Orchard. Leo Fanshawe was a friend of Mr Box and lived in a large house close by. The Fanshawes had been in India and Mrs Fanshawe had corrugated skin like a tortoise which our mother said was because of the sun..

Their son, Simon, was a nasty boy who told tales, and it was open warfare between us and him. He was away at Eton most of the time, so we didn't see him much.

Scrumping in the Fanshawes' orchard may sound tame, but it was close to their house and so a pretty big dare. We didn't need apples, there were plenty in our own orchard, though not these delicious little brown russets.

I had been put on look-out duty on the fence while Pat and Tommy did the actual scrump. The milkman came by.

'Hallo, young Eileen, what are you up to?'

'I'm the Lookout,' I'd said importantly, tossing my plaits.

'Better not tell me any more then,' he'd laughed.

He was no friend of the Fanshawes, who were always late paying their bills and never gave him a Christmas tip. I'd overheard him grumbling about them to my mother one day. Pat and Tommy emerged from the orchard triumphantly, their jerseys bulging.

'It's so easy,' they boasted, 'we could even build a camp in there.'

'Yes, Pat, but we wouldn't do that, would we?' asked Tommy nervously. 'It'd be too dangerous. I've got to go home now. Mum gets cross if I'm late.'

'Course, if you're too scared,' said Pat

And so we made a small camp in one of the trees and munched our way through the best russets for most of the summer. We wrote a Log, like Real Spies, and recorded the comings and goings of the Fanshawes household. Armstrongs the Wine Merchant was the most frequent visitor.

Then Simon came home from his summer holiday staying with a school chum in Nice, and it was all up.

Our parents were furious, which was unusual because they rarely ever were, and allowed us a very free rein. With hindsight I can understand why. It was the class thing. *Their* children *stealing* from their employer's friend.

'You and Tommy will have to go and apologise,' our father said sternly to Pat.

Turning to me he said, 'And you will go to bed early all this week.'

'Wigs has got to come, too,' Pat said 'She's in it just as much as us.'

'No, she's too young,' our father said firmly. This condemned me to a far worse punishment - that of Pat's unknown reprisal and possible banishment from the Gang!

I lay wide-awake in our shared bedroom, listening to the summer sounds coming up from the garden. The sun was shining and it wasn't fair.

Much later, Pat came up to bed and told me what had happened. At Timberhorne Manor, Pat and Tommy had shuffled on the front door step and looked at the huge iron bell pull.

'You go first.'

'Why?'

'Because you're bigger than me.'

'But you're a girl.'

Finally they had both rang the bell together and Leo Fanshawe answered it, holding a glass in his hand. He had seemed surprised to see them.

'My Mummy and Daddy said I had to say I'm sorry,' said Pat.

'Oh, you're the little Roffey girl. Ah yes, apples wasn't it? Er, well, don't do it again then. Bad Show,' he said and closed the door.

From an upstairs window they had seen Simon pulling faces and laughing.

Years later I encountered Simon again when he was the defendant in a rather nasty harassment case. As a Magistrate, it helps to have a good memory for names.

Eileen

DECEMBER
The Broken Angel

The small conservatory was dressed for Christmas; the angel at the top of the tree, wounded in an earlier nativity, had one original glass wing and two inferior plastic jobs; a three-winged emblem for a twenty-first century Christmas.

'If one more person asks me what we will be eating on Christmas Day, I shall scream,' said Elaine.

'Tell them you're having a vulture, stuffed with a humming bird, that should shut them up,' said Eve.

'I know it can all get too much, but there are special moments, moments to remember.' said Julie.

'Tell us,' they chorused.

Silent Night

It's Christmas Eve.

I love this night. It is full of anticipation of the pleasures to come and these start with the song, 'As we climb the stairs...' The ceremony of hanging the stockings on the bed-rails, the numerous 'Good night, but I'm not tired,' and the final 'Father Christmas won't come if you're not asleep.'

In the kitchen the cupboard is full of naughty calories and the fridge is bulging with party goodies, turkey and ham.

My floured fingers knead the pastry trimmings and the smell of mince pies wafts from the oven.

Upstairs, the excited voices stop.

The house has become quiet, like the eye of a storm.

From the garage, two special presents take pride of place in front of the Christmas tree, a doll's house and a skateboard.

In the flickering firelight the room mellows and the tree lights enhance the colourful wrappings.

Christmas carols fill the air.

This is a time for us.

In the quietness, we toast, 'Peace and goodwill, Happy Christmas.'

Julie

A Second Present

'I expect to see a nice drawing when we come back. Remember, Elizabeth, don't answer the door or the phone. I've locked the back door. And I forbid you to go into the other rooms; you're to stay in the kitchen, no wandering around the house.' Sylvia looked at her daughter sternly.

'Yes, Mummy, I'll be good.' Mummy wasn't fun any more, she was always tired and grumpy.

'Come on, Freddy, we'll be late for your appointment.'

The little boy, nursing a swollen right cheek, said, 'I don't want to go to the dentist, Mummy, he's horrible, he breathes all over me; it's all pepperminty, ugh.'

'That tooth will have to come out; you want to be able to eat your Christmas dinner, don't you?' She grabbed his hand and pulled him towards the front door.

Elizabeth listened intently. She heard the sound of the car moving off down the gravelled drive. She looked at the kitchen clock; plenty of time. She worked furiously at the drawing. A snowman, a robin, holly bushes; that would do. Where was her present? She would have to find it today; soon all the presents would be wrapped and it would be too late.

The top of the wardrobe in her parents' bedroom revealed only fluff and dust; the back of the wardrobe, hidden amongst the shoes, yielded a promising haul of two large brown paper sacks, but it was only Freddy's presents: a silly Action Man and a new football and boots. I expect he'll break a window on Christmas day, Elizabeth thought, and then Mummy and Daddy will lose their tempers and shout at each other. Wish I had a sister.

In the big chest of drawers there were clothes and mothballs, no presents. Elizabeth, frustrated, wandered onto the landing. She looked at the linen chest; it wouldn't be there, too easy. There was only Daddy's study left. She was smacked the last time she'd poked around in there. She hesitated, ran down the stairs, checked the kitchen clock and, gritting her teeth, turned the big, brass door-knob and pushed open the mahogany door. She looked around. It would have to be in the bureau, which would be locked, but she knew where Daddy kept the key.

She pulled open the last drawer, a big, deep one. Hurrah! But the bag was squashy. Not clothes! She pulled out the contents; there were two bags inside the big one. It was a nightie. She sighed with relief. It was a present for Mummy. It was pink, with puff sleeves and a Peter Pan collar and there was a matching pink bed jacket, with feather trim. Horrible, Mummy would like it.

She opened the second bag. Another nightie! It was short, made of black lace, with satin straps, a naughty nightie. She didn't think Mummy would like this.

She found her present in the garage, hidden in a chest. It was what she had wanted most in all the world.

The presents had been opened after they came back from church. Elizabeth had feigned delighted surprise at the large wooden box containing real paints, reams of proper paper and lots of pencils with sharp, black ends. Freddy was in the garden chasing the football round the shrubs. Mummy and Daddy were smiling at each other over glasses of sherry.

'Thank you, Edward, it's a lovely nightgown, I shall save it for the holidays.'

'Did you like the other one, Mummy?' Elizabeth gasped and covered her mouth with a trembling hand. A guilty blush spread to the roots of her brown curls.

'What do you mean, 'other one'? You've done it again, haven't you? I thought I'd cured you of prying. Tell me at once, what do you mean? Another nightgown?'

'I'm sorry, Mummy, but I didn't think you'd like it; it was black, you could see through it, it was like one naughty ladies wear.' Elizabeth watched through brown, tear-filled eyes as her mother turned on her father.

'So it has come to this, has it, Edward. I know I haven't been… but I've been tired, run down. But how could you buy an article like that for someone else?'

'Sylvia, let me explain…'

'Did you or did you not buy this disgusting piece of apparel?'

'Well, yes, but it's not disgusting…'

'I demand to know who you bought it for.'

'I bought it for you, my darling.'

'For me, then pray where is this garment?'

'It's under your pillow, I was hoping you would wear it tonight.'

Sylvia imitated her daughter's action and, crimson-faced, rushed from the room. Elizabeth heard her feet pounding up the stairs; she decided that she would stay quiet as a mouse and perhaps they would forget all about her prying.

Her mother entered the room and flew into her father's arms. 'Eddy, darling, please forgive me.' Elizabeth watched as they kissed passionately. Ugh.

'You've given me an extra present, Sylvia. I'm quite chuffed you could be so jealous.' They kissed again, even harder this time.

Daddy turned to her. 'Your mother's feeling a bit tired, we're going to lie down for half an hour. Be good, look after Freddy.'

'Don't open the oven. You can have the TV on if you want.' Her mother smiled at her dreamily. Arms entwined they made their way up the stairs.

'Where's Mum and Dad? They'll kill you if they catch you watching cartoons.' Freddy had entered the sitting room in his muddy boots. Elizabeth pointed to them and to the lumps of earth scattered on the carpet. 'They'll kill me as well,' he sighed and started to tiptoe out of the room.

'Don't worry, Freddy. We can do what we like today, we won't get told off.'

'Why, have they gone out?'

'No, they're upstairs.' She rolled her eyes and made kissing noises.

'Great, shall we eat some sweets?' He joined her on the settee and after demolishing chocolate bon-bons and a packet of toffee curls, they decide to have a fight with the cushions.

Sylvia and Edward found them asleep on the settee. Sweet wrappers had mixed with the mud on the carpet and all around and over them was a light covering of what seemed to be snow, but on closer examination proved to be downy feathers. They looked at each other and laughed.

'I'll see to the dinner; would you mind tidying them up? Don't scold, it *is* Christmas.'

Vera

The Last Christmas

Everything was ready and she was dead tired, but not too tired to be afraid. What would he find fault with, what not to his liking, and what sort of mood would he be in when he came home? It wasn't six o'clock yet, too early to have a drink - but then it was nearly Christmas and she'd been very good lately, so perhaps a small whisky ... Anne had long forgotten what a small whisky measured since she preferred to pour her own, and they were never small. The great thing about alcohol, she thought, was that it helped you relax and let go. It was a long time since she'd done that. She remembered her leaving party at Dalton Marine where she'd kept both the books and the men in some sort of order. She'd missed them after she left, but Robert had said it wasn't in keeping for her to have a clerk's job with his new position. Funny, she'd never thought of her job in that way. It had been fun and people seemed to like her and value what she did.

The house gleamed. Lights from the impeccable non-drop Christmas tree glowed discreetly in the corner of the drawing room. A ready-made table decoration took centre stage on the dining table.

The food had been delivered from Waitrose that afternoon, already arranged on festive platters. All that Anne had to do was warm a few things just before the guests arrived. Surely she could manage to do that? *Let us take the Strain, While you Entertain.* Fine, but it hadn't been a strain when she was small. One Christmas, Mum had dropped a whole tin of roast potatoes that had slid greasily over the kitchen floor while Dad had been plying her with Whisky Macs.

'Gotta keep the cook's strength up,' he'd laughed. 'Nothing wrong with *my* strength,' she'd thrown back at him. 'It's *yours* you've gotta watch out for.'

Anne hadn't understood then, but they had both seemed very happy.

She was not, in this now unequal marriage where status and appearances seemed to matter so much to Robert. Anne didn't know where she fitted in any more. And the harder she tried, the angrier he became. Anne always blamed herself. But why would it matter if the needles dropped? Mrs Ainsley would be here in the morning to restore everything to normal. It was Robert's insistence that she needed help in the house, because she couldn't possibly cope, wouldn't manage it.

'After all' he'd said, tapping numbers into his mobile and not looking at her 'you need to be on hand if I need you ...'

It was never clear to Anne what she could possibly be on hand for in Robert's business, since he didn't trust her to get things right. But slowly she realised that it was an entrapment, a way of harnessing her to the house and controlling her movements. The Bully's final way.

Nick arrived, large and warm, and enveloped her in a hug.

'Mum, who have I got to be extra nice to and was I rude to anybody last year and are there any girls coming?'

'No one, and probably not, except that you did tell Judy Bass that modern fiction was dead and she's the local author, - and yes, I think there are some daughters of sorts.'

Now she did need a drink. They would all be arriving soon. Robert had not yet come. Her stomach knotted and her hand moved towards the bottle. She heard the car pull into the drive, the automatic garage door go up, and the rasp of his key in the lock. Robert strode into the kitchen, already angry. His glance swept round the worktops assessing the situation.

'You're not even dressed yet, they'll be here soon,' he said. 'What in God's name have you been doing all day? And why the white plates instead of the gold- rimmed and I said *I'd* do the dressings.' He turned up the oven unnecessarily.

Anne did not reply but walked slowly past him out of the kitchen. This had to be the last Christmas it would be like this. She went quietly up to the bedroom to put on her warmest coat. She collected the bank details and wrote a note for Nick. She heard Robert showering in his own bathroom. Downstairs, the salmon canapés were all ready and the vol au vents were warming in the oven. She had a final drink from the half-bottle behind the biscuit tin and put it in her handbag. She wouldn't let him have the final triumph of finding it there. Leaving through the back door, she locked it and posted the key through the flap. She would not be needing it any more.

'Where to, my lovely?' asked the bus driver.
'Where are you going?'
'We're circular – we come back to the same place, luv.'
'That won't do,' she said.
And it didn't.

It was some time before she was missed.

Eileen

Night Visitors

At last, out of the cold and biting wind into the almost hothouse atmosphere of the apartment high above the streets of Budapest. I peel off layers of clothing and remove my boots in the hall before going into the kitchen to turn on the kettle. Whilst waiting for the water to boil, I wander through to the bedroom and slip into something casual, returning to the kitchen to make a large mug of honeyed peppermint tea. I settle down on the sofa in the sitting room to enjoy my drink.

Picking up the control from the coffee table, I flick through the TV channels until one, a local news station, holds my interest. Scenes of the Danube, flowing slowly with large chunks of ice floating on top, a few shots of buildings and squares with people picking their way along the snow covered streets, intent on getting indoors as soon as possible.

Now I see the man I've just passed, huddled in the phone booth just around the corner and a man ladling what looks like soup into a mug held by a woman, who is talking to the first man. Then from a stainless steel canister they heap a plastic container with pasta and from a bag the woman hands him a piece of bread and a spoon. Flashes of these two stalwart, well-wrapped people are shown in various parts of the city handing out food and blankets to the homeless, none of them young. The couple have stopped again, literally on the street behind this building. I recognise the wooden structure with a roof to protect pedestrians from falling masonry.

A news reporter appears on the screen and talks with the industrious couple and, although I don't speak Hungarian, I gather they visit the homeless every night.

The scene changes to the Opera House, a magical place. Switching off the TV and returning to the hall, I put back on all the layers of clothing and, emptying coins from a jar into a plastic bag, I rush out of the door, down in the lift and out into the cold night.

Round the corner there are two huddled bundles in the doorway, the wooden construction giving them extra shelter. Now what to do? I don't want to startle them.

'Hello! Jo-napot! Hello!'

A head comes out from under the covers, wearing a woolly hat. Now another head appears similarly dressed. They are listening to a little radio. These are the men that were here last summer. I remember the radio when I gave them some change. They had not asked for anything and were clean and quite well dressed. They had thanked me and we had laughed but then it was warm and the evenings were long. I place the little bag on the ground in front of them and wish them 'Merry Christmas.' As I turn away a voice calls out in English:

'Thank you. Merry Christmas.'

The next day, with a flurry of snowflakes blowing around me, I pass the spot. The night visitors have gone without a trace.

Elaine

Past Christmases

Jackie and I crouched in terror beneath the dining table. There was this short round old bearded man dressed in red. He was bent low under the weight of the sack on his shoulder and leaned on his stick as he walked into the room, shouting 'Ho! Ho! Ho!' We clung to each other, holding our breath while we peeked out, wide-eyed, from under the white tablecloth, which hung almost to the ground.

This is one of my earliest recollections of Christmas. Of course, it was only Grandpa and he was such a kind man – but the memory of the fear has remained with me to this day. That Christmas, we were given little blue and scarlet metal tricycles and allowed to pedal round the house – an unheard of privilege in that austere Victorian household! Standards were slipping.

The last time our children holidayed with us was a Christmas spent in Tunisia. Even then it was under protest – but father insisted. The three of them shared a room. The two eldest took the singles and consigned their younger brother to the child's bed. The fact that he was the biggest made no difference; his head hung over one end and his feet the other. The weather was cold and windy. We haggled for warm djellabahs in the souk. The boys tried bartering their sister for a few camels and a goat - or was it a donkey? They left the hotel dining-room embarrassed by their parents' romantic dancing and they buried their couscous in the sand at a beach BBQ one cold evening,

Another Christmas well remembered by our children. Their father had been in hospital for some time but was allowed home for the festivities. Some festivities! He lay in pain on the sofa for the few days before returning to hospital. My mother spent the day moribund as usual in her wheelchair –

she had suffered several strokes and her speech was impaired, so she sat and cried for my husband, a first – they were not the greatest of friends. My aunts came. One had damaged her knee and could barely walk. All a big nightmare, though I suppose I must have fed and entertained everyone. It is known as The Geriatric Christmas.

My first Christmas with my boyfriend's family was a challenge to see how much could be piled on my plate by his aunt. It has remained a source of amusement to them and embarrassment to me that I couldn't, no matter how hard I tried, or how much they cheered me on, clear my plate. Perhaps this was a test to see if I were acceptable to this family of 'mighty appetites'? Should I have cut and run?

Christmases abroad as young marrieds were one big round of parties: visiting each other's homes, celebrating in the Club, drinking, eating and dancing. An added interest was having your turkey gobbling away in your backyard before the big event. The whisky poured down his (and the cook's) throat softened the blow when it came, we believe. Finding ingredients for puddings and cakes took some ingenious bribery and corruption. James decorated cakes with the help of three Sudanese gangers who'd never seen anything like it in their lives. Neither had I!

In Sierra Leone, James spent a Christmas without me and was entertained to three festive meals in twenty-four hours with only short naps and long swims in the sea to replenish his appetite and lower his alcohol content between them. A French family cooked him goose on Christmas Eve, waking their small children at midnight to open their presents. Apparently they might then sleep late on Christmas morning – a vain hope in my experience. He was regaled with a full English Christmas dinner with another family and yet a third insisted he came for their meal in the evening. Had the makers of the *Vicar of Dibley* heard about him?

Apart from no-one wishing to leave him on his own at Christmas, these invitations were also to thank him for acting as baby-sitter-in-chief in the compound. One small child if woken was in the habit of walking through to his parents' bed, where his mother would join him until he settled down again. James, of course, did as he was bid and lay on the bed with Johnny on the evening of a thunderstorm. It took a long time for him to live down the rumour spread by little Johnny that 'Uncle James had slept in Mummy's bed.'

Eve

JANUARY
Making themselves at Home

As soon as they entered the conservatory they rearranged the furniture, placing two tables together. The girl from the bar switched on the heating; she was as pleasant and as welcoming and as puzzled as the rest of the staff by the five who came once a month and spent several hours reading stories and laughing. They felt at home, and so they talked about their homes.

Gravesend – 1958

Only ten days before our wedding, a real homemade affair. My future mother-in-law was a tailoress, and even the men's suits were bespoke - but where were we to live? We had looked at some weird accommodation, furnished and unfurnished, without success and were becoming very despondent when, out of the blue, a flat-mate's estate agent father came up with 5 Crossley Avenue, Gravesend. This 1930s unfurnished terrace house was ours to rent – a whole house and garden!

'Gravesend-on-Mud' was an ideal location for James's contract at Crossness and doubtless I would find work nearby. Family and friends offered their cast-off furniture, which we eagerly accepted, hired a lorry and traipsed round collecting a deal chair from here, a bed from there, a faded carpet, a dining-table and so on. My brother was not impressed by my fiancé's lorry-driving but we survived. Some items we picked up at auctions; a three-piece moquette suite in fawn and black (ghastly), two birds'-eye-maple wardrobes and dressing table with triptych mirror (not much better), a small bureau (the best of a bad bunch). Together with wedding presents, the contents of my bottom drawer and a few old curtains, rugs and cushions we set up home.

The in-laws and James, were DIY enthusiasts, not something my family went in for. I soon learned that Sunday mornings were not for lie-ins, even for newly-weds. The in-laws' Austin would stop outside our gate with a flourish of horn blowing and re-decorating would begin. It was all the rage to have three walls of one colour, contrasting with the fourth. Dell Boy would have been proud of our little sitting room with its three pale green walls, bamboo pattern on a black background papered fourth wall. A black skirting board and picture rail covered the original dark brown paint admirably.

Our six-foot table just fitted diagonally across the dining room and here I flippantly suggested it would be odd if people papered their walls with newspaper – but it might help with subjects for conversation over a meal. The newsagent delivered *The Financial Times* for a fortnight. We glued it on higgledy-piggledy and matched the pink for the other three walls. Scarlet paint covered the deep brown skirting boards and picture rails.

One dark evening, a fire engine came to a screaming halt outside. To his horror James could see flickering through the open bedroom door. With his heart in his mouth, he leapt up the stairs – only to find the fire engine's lights reflecting through the window of our newly decorated room.

It snowed that winter. What did the neighbours think of us dashing into the back garden, throwing handfuls of snow and chasing each other out of the back gate, round the end of the terrace and in through the front door, shouting and laughing as we ran? The neighbours were elderly and, hopefully, deaf as well.

We had no car, but during that first year of our marriage, James (but I think mostly his father) managed to buy Sular, an airborne lifeboat, from somewhere near Shillingford Bridge. These long narrow vessels were dropped from bombers to shipwrecked sailors during the Second World War. It was his first essay into boat owning which was to continue for the next half century! One bank holiday weekend, he and I started on the long trip down the Thames to Gravesend. With just a tarpaulin for cover, we took a soaking from time to time. We had to put into Henley-on-Thames overnight when the engine failed; the petrol tank had more perforations than a sieve. Little did I know then, I'd end up living nearby. Coming through London, we pulled towards Westminster Pier only to be shouted at by a policeman. I yelled back, 'I've got to go to the loo'. Nonplussed and embarrassed, he allowed us to moor up.

Our stay in Gravesend was not to last. The following autumn, James was offered a contract in Port Sudan and by Christmas Day we were setting up home again. In fact, over the next ten years we were destined to move home as one contract ended and another began; from Port Sudan to Khartoum, on to Guneid, then Freetown; back to England as first time home-owners in Keston, Kent, then south west to Creedy Barton, north to Northwich, and finally, Henley-on-Thames.

Eve

The Caretakers

The Garden Flat on the south side of Clapham Common had a proud tradition of sheltering couples who Lived In Sin. That is what it was called in the 1970s when you lived together. Caz and Ed, who worked in the packing department of the Army and Navy Stores, had passed the flat to Jill and James, who in turn had passed it to us.

'I can't possibly ever do it and I'm amazed you should ask,' I said.

'But it's only till we get married in December and I'm fed up with hitching lifts every night across London,' he said.

'Precisely. It's not the sin bit but the fact that you expect me to live in *South* London,' I said. 'That's across the river!'

'So I'll bribe the Ferryman,' he said.

The flat had originally been a potting shed (my version) of a very grand house, which was now divided into huge flats, occupied by hundreds of people. They rarely met but left each other vitriolic notes in milk bottles: *Will the lousy bastard who keeps pinching my milk kindly go buy their own.*

The Garden Flat was a bedsitter with bits on. It also had a fridge, a telephone and a kitchen with a wooden worktop and bath underneath. You had to duck to avoid cuphooks when getting out and we could open the front door from the bed. The cooker was unspeakable, held together with grease. I realised that I'd made a wise choice in Life Partner when I found him with all its grisly parts laid out on the lawn as if for a surgical operation.

'Do you know how to put them back?' I asked.

He gave me a withering look before replying. 'Well if not, the government wasted its money on five years' engineering training.'

'Yes, but on gas stoves?' I always liked to have the last word.

Our landlord, Giles Tindall-Carter, was a gentleman farmer from Dorset whose wife had inherited the house. Every month he was sent to do his landlord bit and report to her on the state of house and tenants. He would perch uncomfortably in hot corduroys on the end of our bed and complain bitterly about the other tenants, particularly the medical students from Barts who had the flat above ours. They were always late with the rent, if they paid at all. His unannounced visits necessitated the swift transition of my Woollies ring from handbag to wedding finger.

On one of his misery tours, he proposed that as we were the only 'married couple' would we consider being unofficial caretakers in lieu of rent? Oh, would we! Duties involved keeping the garden tidy and *polishing* the hall. This he impressed upon us was extremely important to his wife, perhaps as a reminder of her family's former glory. South London Mercury and Final Reminders from Clapham Unigate were strewn there most days, but it was rent-free so we agreed to polish away.

Now, as unofficial keepers of the house dustbins, we were able legitimately to ransack them for empties from med students' parties. These returns produced after lengthy but rewarding tours of Clapham Common's twenty-seven pubs - enough for a bottle of Emva Cream or a curry at Rajput South.

Then came November storms. Dustbins were tossed like toys and contents strewn over the lawn. As Caretakers we had prioritised and did not polish the Great Hall of Clapham. Unfortunately, this coincided with a rare visit from Mrs

Tindall-Carter, and we were sacked. We didn't care as we were getting married anyway in two weeks time; leaving South Side to cross the Common to an unfurnished flat in Balham.

In the meantime, those naughty Barts boys had not paid their rent and he was taking them to court for non-payment.

'Not what you would expect from boys of good families,' Farmer Tindall-Carter had reflected sadly. We didn't bother to tell him that these Nice Boys had peeing competitions over their balcony into the garden, but that most of it landed on our leaky flat roof beneath. The rush mats were totally ruined.

'Anyway,' he said gloomily, 'the court date is 16th December and I need you to attend to give evidence.'

The 16th December was our Wedding Day!

But it all ended happily. The med students flitted two days before the trial. We got married and I still have two rings. One is a bit green.

Eileen

The Hollies

Our first home was on the outskirts of Lincoln, a city dominated by its great Cathedral. As we drove into the driveway of the double-fronted Victorian house, a large friendly lady of about sixty opened the door. She welcomed Michael and I in and gave us tea in her drawing room. Then we were shown the rooms we would be renting, a bedroom, a sitting-room and a bathroom at the end of the landing.

Next day, having unpacked our belongings, Michael drove off to RAF Scampton, his first posting, and I ventured into town on the bus. I returned to The Hollies a few hours later, laden with groceries. I had also bought a large heavy frying-pan, which the salesman said was a good investment at a guinea and would last a lifetime, and a paperback copy of *Lady Chatterley's Lover*, which I started to read immediately. Needless to say Michael was not impressed by my extravagant purchase, the frying pan, which I have to this day, forty-five years later, just as I was not impressed with the paperback, long since lost on our travels.

Due to Michael's shift work at the camp, I would spend many evenings on my own. I decided to investigate the job front. I persuaded the theatre in Lincoln to employ me as a jack of all trades. I settled in, helping with props, stage management, prompt, taking small parts, sometimes with a few lines and got hauled into anything with song and dance. However, what I enjoyed most was being able to watch productions from front of house when selling programmes and ice creams.

After a few weeks our landlady informed us that she was going to visit her sister who lived on a bulb farm near Spalding. Her cleaner would continue to come twice a week and neighbours, who had a spare key, would assist with any problems. The house seemed very large now, with the grandfather clock on the landing keeping watch.

As a young couple, we became involved with entertainment on the camp (famous for 617 Squadron - the Dambusters) and drove around the countryside, which was flat and uninteresting. I remember being devastated on visiting Gainsborough to find a miserable town with closed down factories. We made several friends and, one, a keen young journalist did a front-page interview, with photograph. It ended rather lamely as when asked what inspired me about Lincolnshire, I replied, 'the church spires'.

The 1960-61 winter was harsh and, more than once, I fell flat on my face in the deep snow pushing the car to get it started. Our landlady returned for a few days before departing to visit her son in South Africa. Shortly afterwards we, too, departed for a posting in the sun, one of many. Although I have had many homes over the years, memories of our first home, The Hollies, never fade.

Elaine

What is a Home?

Home, what is a home? Is it a house you live in? I've been to other children's homes: there's a Mum and a Dad, brothers and sisters, it's noisy, the radio is playing, people talk to each other, they laugh, they quarrel over toys, someone cries; the mother hands out a slap, a hug, a kiss, a jam sandwich. I stand and watch them; it's confusing, so many children, so much noise.

I had a home. There was a mother, a father, Joey the budgerigar and me. It was a warm and happy home. I made scones in bottle tops; I picked the yellow coltsfoot in the field; father gave me Toblerone and grapes. He had a woollen jersey with a zip, I pulled it up and down, we laughed together. I loved Joey. We hid together under the table at night, Joey in his cage and me in my siren suit, we could hear the planes over head. When I was in the bath in front of the fire, he would fly around the room and land on my head. I was happy.

Then it wasn't a home any more. It was a place to visit. It was cold. My mother would polish the furniture and she would sigh. Where was my father?

I was planting seeds in the tiny back garden; there was a man on a ladder, mending tiles on the roof. He had a white beard like Father Christmas.

'Why are you sighing so much, little girl?' I looked at him. He had bright blue eyes. Why did he ask? Is sighing wrong?

We lived with Granny and Granddad until I was seven. Every week we visited the house and every week we visited my father's grave: to empty the slimy urn of its dead flowers, to wash the golden letters on the black stone; to open the stiff windows and let out the stale air, to touch the cold furniture with its silvery bloom.

When my grandparents died we moved to Suffolk to live with my mother's sister and her husband. My mother gave up the house. I was glad, I didn't like going there, it was cold and sad. Our furniture came with us to help fill the tall, thin, five-storey building; a shop below, a boarding house above. The house did not become home; the beach, the sea, the marshes made me welcome, they were my home.

My cousin and her husband rented our old house and, when we came back to visit at Christmas, the house was warm and cosy, full of life and love. I was happy for the house, it was alive again. Once more it was a home.

Vera

Those Were the Years

Hi there, I'm a touring caravan called Bailey.

I heard them say they are going to retire me. I'm to be banished from my spot, where I have stood for the past thirty years. If I could cry tears, I would fill a bucket in five minutes. I'm not worn out. I've given them good service, no leaks and no draught holes. Four or five, comfortable beds. *And,* I've put up with all those cooking smells; she's a thrifty lady, doesn't believe in eating out.

He tried to set me on fire one year, when a pair of his model plane wings was left over the gaslight. And what about those bikes I've had wiggled through my narrow door and tied to my coat hooks?

I've been towed round England, Scotland, Wales and every country in Europe.

Never once did a tail wag, when he was bounding along the motorway at sixty miles an hour. It's all in the packing, so I heard him say; get the centre of gravity right, whatever that might mean.

Mind you, we did do a jack-knife in a muddy Welsh campsite and dent my left front corner. Gosh, did that hurt! So did the hammering to straighten it out.

I'm sounding all moans. There were the lovely hot days that followed near Harlech Castle. Heaven for me, she cooked outside.

I must mention one foggy, *pea soup* foggy, night in Scotland. They couldn't find the site. I was being shunted to a stop every few yards and the voices inside the car were getting louder. Suddenly I was swung into a lay-by and my aching body relaxed only when they fell into their bunks to sleep. I'm a martyr to the bumping treatment I get.

The next morning was a different world – blue sky, sun – and we were only yards away from the campsite! Halstead's Farm and Museum, at Hadrian's Wall. I won't go into what was said.

Later, I couldn't believe my windows when they brought a kitten inside me. It was a longhaired ginger tom with a white-ringed tail. It was half farm, half wild cat! Had they gone mad? They left it in a box on my table! I was very careful not to bump along the narrow roads, but that did depend on how skilful he was until we joined the motorway south.

Puss and I became great travelling partners over the next ten years, and he always sat on the table and looked out of the front window.

And of course there was the time…

What's that? I'm her lovely little home from home; I've got so many memories she can't do it. Is this a reprieve? They want to have me swung into the air, over the roof and land in the garden. They must be stark raving bonkers!

It's the only way, or I'm out on my tyres behind the first rag and bone van that comes along.

Bring on the lifting gear. I can't wait to be a summerhouse.

Julie

FEBRUARY
Cauliflower cheese

There was no sign of the vine breaking bud; they wondered if it was possible for life to lurk beneath the dry, twisting ropes which snaked over the roof of the conservatory.

Eileen decided to order cauliflower cheese. The other four decided they too would like cauliflower cheese. 'Why is it,' said Eileen, 'that when one person firmly states a preference, all the others, who have been orming about, suddenly decide they too must have the same?' After they philosophised on this conundrum for several minutes, Elaine commented on the handsome cream candles on the tables.

'A gift, perhaps?' she said.

'Double-edged swords, gifts,' stated Vera. They gave her questioning looks and so she explained.

Disaster from the USA

It was Christmas, 1949. We were huddled around the kitchen grate, staring at a large cardboard box, which boldly carried on its surface the sender's address – Michigan, USA. Christmas presents from our recently emigrated relatives to their poor relations in Suffolk.

Boxes of exotica: Hershey bars, chocolates stuffed with cherries, popcorn, tins of meat. Saliva dribbled from our rationed-booked mouths.

A parcel just for me? Happy Christmas, Vera. Would it be toys, better still, books? I was helped to unpack the parcel. Clothes - oh no!

A white blouse with broderie anglaise frills across the chest and around the three-quarter length sleeves; a neat collar with

A BLACK BOW. A red felt flared skirt with two white PUPPY DOGS chasing a big MUMMY DOG across the bottom; all with their red tongues out and wearing CUTE LITTLE COLLARS. To complete the ensemble, a red, leather belt embellished with brass buckles with ANOTHER perky pooch in the centre. I loved dogs, but I didn't want to wear them.

I was nine, tall for my age, painfully thin; I was not a pretty child. This outfit called out for Shirley Temple, not Jane Eyre.

My mother and aunt drooled over the clothes. I was to have my photograph taken by the town's top professional, copies to be sent to the relatives, copies for everyone.

I was dragged to the studio. My thick, fair hair was tied into two bunches with white ribbons. In embarrassed, sullen silence I was paraded before the photographer in the ghastly clothes.

'Smile,' said the photographer. No movement of the lips. 'Smile, come on, dear, do try to smile.' He ordered my mother from the room.

The photograph I look at today shows a slight, wry smile, no sign of teeth; the eyes are looking outwards, there is a glint of amusement, as though a secret has been shared. He was kind to me by cutting off the photograph below the hem of the skirt, thus preventing my stick-like legs from appearing. The three dogs are still running around the red felt, wishing they had been sent to some cheery cherub who would have loved them.

Vera

Mirror into the Past

We all have things that are precious and personal to us. How could I pick out something that is extra special to me and may hold some wider interest? I choose my still life, now on the wall of our bedroom. It is about twelve by eighteen inches, a vase of roses in full bloom, petals about to drop, painted in oils in the style of one of the old Dutch Masters, dark background, nondescript vase but the flowers have a lifelike iridescent quality - a pleasing picture in a battered frame. Family and friends comment on the charming painting but agree that the awful frame has certainly seen better days.

We spent three years in Libya in the late '60s and lived on the third floor of an apartment block, which we reached by lift after getting past the Gaffir. It was always breaking down and I often had to mount the stairs with shopping, pushchair, toddler and child in stages, as Gaffir seemed to be immobile when it came to assisting a mere female. When Michael was on the scene, he ran upstairs with the pushchair, Old Uncle Tom Cobbley and all!

Having a Gaffir made our home secure and as the owners of the building lived on the top floor there were never any problems other than at Eid (Muslim Holiday) when live sheep travelled up in the lift, never to be seen again!

A few yards from the building was a shopping complex, with grocery store, newsagents and an art gallery. A few days before my birthday, Michael asked what I would like and, on passing this gallery, I spotted a picture in the window and remarked:

'I'd like that little picture,' I told him. 'It reminds me of home but not in that hideous frame.'

The gallery was a hive of industry. The men, taking pictures down off the walls, did not seem interested in selling the picture, which was quite expensive, even less so when we asked for a simple frame and said that we were in no hurry for it to be made.

'It's my wife's birthday in two days and she would really like this picture.'

Three young men went into a huddled conversation and one came across to us and said:

'Fine. Come back this evening, nine o'clock. Pay then.'

The picture was collected and paid for by Michael who was not really satisfied with the workmanship, but I was delighted.

The next day we found the gallery shut and empty. Later that day the border with Egypt was closed, which answered our question as to why the young men were in such a hurry to give us the picture. They were anxious to leave Libya and get over the border to Egypt and home to their families.

Every time I look at my little picture it takes me back to Libya, rekindling memories of that time and reminding me that riches in life are given through the kindness of people.

Elaine

A Band of Gold
- Or what Mothers never tell

First the gift of the diamond ring.

'Oh! How wonderful, you're engaged,' chorus the girlie friends.

'Well, you're on your way now. Just the little band of gold to come,' coos mother.

Days of shopping for the perfect gown. Wedding presents arriving day by day. Enough towels to last a lifetime, and a Chinese vase that will never see the light of day. But lots of useful dishes, pots and pans; some folks remembered their list.

The Day arrives. He slips the band of gold onto her finger, his gift of love.

Year one is the paper anniversary.

    She got baby congratulation cards. He got a cigar.

Year two is cotton.

    Hubby was being cautious, bought a high-neck nightie.

Come year three, it's leather.

    Money's a bit short. A pair of new shoes would be nice.

Year four is fruit or flowers.

    Doubled as an offering as he walked for the second time down the Maternity Ward.

Year five is wood.

    The new garden shed was a place for him to hide.

Six, seven, eight and nine.

    Passed in a flash with Beaver Cubs' and Brownies' camps.

Year ten is tin.

> The chicken coop fell down. Frozen birds filled the freezer for months.

Eleven is steel.

> This was a black time. The factory closed down.

Sexy twelve and thirteen quotes silk and lace.

> Forget that! Teenage tantrums took their place.

Fourteen is ivory.

> He searched until...A trio of elephants sits on the windowsill.

Fifteen years.

> Where has the time gone? Oh! A beautiful crystal necklace. Where did the money come from?

Twenty years is China.

> What can he come up with for that? Maybe a Spaniel to sit on the hearth? Or a dinner service? No.
>
> Her precious has a ticket for two, so they can walk hand in hand, along the Great *China* Wall.

Julie

Ben's Gift

Daddy-Jo – the nickname for their grandfather – was in hospital. Ben, aged seven, was very worried – Daddy-Jo was old. Was he going to die like Nana had not so long ago? That was really horrid and Daddy had been so sad and angry for ages and ages. Maybe he could make Daddy-Jo a present, which would make him feel better.

He often painted with Mummy. She liked working on silk but suggested he tried painting a picture on a polo shirt for Daddy-Jo. What would he like? Ben decided he would cheer up if he had a picture of his sailing boat, called *Cold Feet*. Could he remember what Daddy-Jo's boat looked like? He drew two good-sized triangles for the sails and filled in the mast and booms with yellow. Cold feet need Wellingtons – so he drew a pair of black ones on the mainsail. The hull was white with a blue line round it; that wasn't too hard. The portholes were a bit tricky; drawing circles was difficult and they came out different sizes. Never mind, everyone knew what they were. Now for the cold feet: he drew them carefully on the hull and coloured them in red. That's the colour his feet went when they were cold. A red flag on the back and the boat was finished. Now for the sea – he didn't want to use the same blue as the line on the hull. The only other blue Mummy had in these special paints was navy, so a wide wiggly line of navy blue it had to be. There was still room for a bright yellow sun and some seagulls on one shoulder. To finish the picture he added a compass, just a cross with the letters N, E, S and W. Mummy told him where they went. He would remember 'Never Eat Shredded Wheat'. He carefully painted his name at the bottom and stood back to admire his work. Daddy-Jo's sure to like this, he thought.

Now what! Josh, his younger brother, wanted to do one as well. OK, but he'd need some help. Josh decided a message would please Daddy-Jo and, using his favourite colour – blue – he copied the words, 'We love you Daddy-Jo,' in a big bold scrawl across the front and drew some hearts with faces in them. For a bit more colour, he added a large scarlet splurge down one side. That didn't take long, thought Josh and raced back to his favourite computer game.

Daddy-Jo didn't look very ill, decided Ben when they went to see him. Maybe he'll be all right after all. He was so happy to see them and he loved his presents. Everyone in the ward admired them too, though the staff nurse asked Daddy-Jo not to wear Josh's in hospital. All that blood would give the ward a bad name!

Eve

A Gift of Bricks

At 4.30 in the morning the twenty-seventh brick came flying through Jane Harbert's bedroom window. It had a message attached with an elastic band. Jane detached it and put it with the other twenty-six messages in a neat pile on her dressing table. It read pretty much the same as the others:

'You cannot live without me and soon you will realise it. I hope you've moved your bed.'

That was why she couldn't possibly go any further with him – a man who thought that you would live beneath a barrage of glass without simple precautions. It offended her that he should so deny a knowledge of Health and Safety, especially her own.

The twenty-five preceding messages spoke of 'great attraction', (good, she liked that), 'desire to see her' (well, of course), and 'she was so different from all the others' (where had he been not to know that?') and so on...

His methods had admittedly been a little extreme, but since after their first meeting she'd refused to answer his phone calls and texts, Jane supposed she should expect that.

From childhood, Jane had always demanded adulation from her suitors. She'd tied up Toby Milne aged seven to a stake in the garden and made him eat a wasp's nest. Actually he'd burst into tears before she could thrust it down his throat, but she felt that it was a small price to pay for showing him her white aertex knickers.

'No Eat, no Peep,' she'd said, and flounced off into the darkening gloom of their enormous garden.

At Oxford, Toby had become a confirmed homosexual and joined the Secret Service giving secrets to the Russians. They had made him eat the equivalent of wasps' nests, but for compensation he had a beautiful view over the Volga.

From her bedroom at the front of the house, Jane saw him unloading next week's supply of bricks. She felt almost moved to go down and offer help, but that might be misconstrued as encouragement.

The elastic bands were obviously recycled from postmen's droppings, and she felt virtuous that she was helping the environment.

Jane was entertaining her mother and sister to dinner on the night that Brick Twenty-Eight came through. The Bedroom Tactics weren't working so it was a Direct Hit into the dining room which felled her mother at once.

The patio was a beautiful configuration of multi-coloured brickwork and much admired at the funeral reception. It was also a high selling-point when she sold the house prior to her marriage to wealthy tycoon Sir Peter Naseby, who had made his fortune in double-glazing.

Eileen

MARCH
Lasagne and a glass of wine

New leaves, pleated and shiny, adorned the grapevine, and embryonic clusters of grapes held promise for the coming summer. The putto in the garden, clutching his dolphin, looked decidedly chipper in the spring sunshine.

'I believe he has developed a smile,' declared Eve.

'Concentrate on the menu,' commanded Julie, 'we're all having fish pie.'

'In that case, I'll have lasagne and a large glass of wine.'

'Celebrating something special?' asked Eileen.

Late Joy

'I don't *want* to go – it smells of old cabbage and cats!' said Sam.

'It does *not*, Sam, that's just your imagination. They don't allow cats in the Eventide Nursing Home.'

'Mrs Jackson's got a Peke. She keeps it in a basket and puts knitting on top of it as a disguise. I saw it last time we visited Gran,' put in Ellie.

'How does she feed it?' Sam asked, temporarily deflected.

'Smuggled leftovers, I think,' said Ellie, 'and one of the kitchen maids sneaks it out for walks when no one's looking.'

Exasperated, Jane regarded her two children. 'No buts,' she said firmly, 'we are *all* going to the Birthday Tea tomorrow and celebrate Gran's ninetieth in style – or I'll tell Matron about the Peke.'

'But, Mum, Gran doesn't want a birthday tea or any other kind of fuss, she told me,' said Sam, his face unusually serious.

'Well, she's having one, like it or not, otherwise she'll complain that no one remembered and that she's better off out of everyone's way and I'm not having *that* laid at my door on top of everything else!'

The two children looked at her shocked. Indeed, she'd shocked herself by words thought, but never said.

'I've bought champagne and a cake from Waitrose,' Jane went on. 'And we'll all take presents.'

'She'd rather have Glenfiddich,' Ellie said. 'Champagne gives her heartburn.'

'And smoked salmon,' went on Sam. 'She doesn't like cake.'

'You both seem to have an intimate knowledge of your Grandmother's tastes,' said Jane sharply.

'Oh, we just talk to her and that,' said Sam. 'Is Dad coming?'

'No of course not, he'll be working,' said Jane.

James would not come anywhere near his mother-in-law if he could possibly avoid it. Just as he forbade her to live with them.

'She smokes in bed – look at that ruined duvet. No, it's simply not on long-term, Jane.' Jane knew he actually did not like the way she made him feel undermined in his own household. The children giggled a lot and Jane ran round after her. No, simply not on.

At the Eventide Nursing Home the nurses were trying to get her ready for the party.

'Let's tart your hair up a bit, Mrs D. I could hot-roller it for you,' offered bouncy Sharon.

'My dear young woman, there's absolutely nothing you can do with five strands of hair and I intend to do my own tarting-up thank you very much.' Daphne pulled out a black knitted woollen hat from the bag on her walking frame and set it on her head at a rakish angle. 'This was knitted for me by a sailor of whom I was extraordinarily fond,' she said dreamily. 'It was while they were becalmed off the Lakshadweep Islands and he knitted it on board on starlit nights and thought longingly of me.'

'Oh Mrs D, that's so romantic,' Sharon said, brown eyes wide in wonder, 'just like in *Bella*.'

Daphne had actually bought it in OXFAM to keep out the draughts in the Day Room but had no intention of telling this mooney young girl. She preferred her own version. There had, in fact, been a sailor but she didn't think he'd done much knitting. Smiling at the memory, she pulled out a red lipstick from her bag and drew a full line over her lips. That would show them!

'Mrs D, you look wonderful,' Matron enthused. 'You'll outlive us all, I shouldn't wonder.'

'That, my dear young woman, is actuarily impossible since you are thirty-two and I am ninety years old. Don't they teach you anything these days?'

The family arrived. Champagne was opened, cake cut and presents presented. Daphne behaved impeccably and was appropriately grateful for her presents although she noticed that her usual annual subscription to *New Encounter* was not amongst them. P'raps they thought it wouldn't be good value, she thought wryly. Jane had given her useful padded garments.

Finally, Sam shuffled up to her looking miserable and holding a small wrapped package.

'I made you this in Woodwork,' he said. 'It started out as a Bear but it went a bit wrong, so now it's a Mouse. Those marks on the side are where its ears would be but they've come off. They're here.' He produced another smaller package from his pocket.

Daphne felt like crying. Her throat closed up and her eyes swam with unaccustomed tears.

'Sam, it's the very best present,' she said. 'Look how he nestles in my hand. I can hold him and think about you. Anyway, ears would have got in the way.'

'Honest?'

'Honest!'

After they'd left, she took the half bottle of Glenfiddich, she'd bribed Sharon to purchase, from her bag and poured a slug. She closed her eyes and smiled as her fingers curled painfully around Mouse. All things considered, it hadn't been so bad after all.

Eileen

Half a Banana

Summer 1945

I knocked loudly on the front door. Gran's footsteps sounded and when the door opened she said, 'There's a special present for you on the table.'

I rushed into the kitchen. In my place was a yellow banana. A *real fruit* banana. Something I had seen only in books! I felt the skin and put it to my nose, sniffing the flavour. It didn't curve as much as the picture book, but I could feel the ridges.

'What do you think of it?' asked Gran, as she put my dinner before me.

'I don't know, I've never had a banana. Not one that I can remember! What does it taste like?'

'Well, it's firm to bite and... tastes lovely.'

'That doesn't tell me what it tastes like.'

'I know. You can take half back to school for afternoon play.'

'And if I like it, I'll have the other half when I come home.'

Through the classroom window, the sun was hot on my back and the brown paper bag beside me. I looked at it many times wondering what it would taste like. Would it be sharp like some of the apples I ate? Or the plums we sometimes received from Mrs Archer? What about Aunt Kate's pears that we helped pick in September? All of these had their own special taste.

Hurry up playtime.

Oh dear, the bottom of the bag is wet. What has happened to my half a banana?

The skin has gone brown and it's squashy. It won't peel! My fingers are all messy and it tastes warm and slimy.

Fish Pie and Laughter

Ugh! I don't like bananas.

It was five years before I tried another one.

Julie

Farewell, Fare Well

For nearly ten years she had stood there. She had become a local landmark but gradually over the years her bright blue and white paintwork dimmed, rust marks dribbled down her sides and lichen slowly crept over her flanks. *Cold Feet* was forty-six foot long and, from the top, it was possible to look into the upstairs windows of the Victorian house whose front garden she occupied.

During all this time, and unbeknown to passers-by, her owner was beavering away building the interior of this hull. Now, on a cold bright February morning, his task was finished, and *Cold Feet* was ready to dip her toes into the sea. Her departure took time to organise - a crane to lift her, a boat transporter to drive her away, another lorry to take her cradle – all to be co-ordinated. It was half-term at the little village school at one end of the lane and no one had arranged to be buried in the churchyard at the other end, so hopefully there wouldn't be other traffic to contend with.

Neighbours were warned that 'essential work made it necessary to cut the power' that morning, so they came to bid farewell to this monument which had graced the village for so long. It became a celebration with a real party atmosphere, either because they were pleased to see the back of her or because the first part of the project had been completed; I didn't ask. People turned up and the mulled wine flowed as the huge crane uprooted and carefully lifted the thirteen-ton vessel over the electricity cables and manoeuvred her on the transporter in the road.

It took some time to get her loaded but then, as she commenced her slow progress, a Landrover appeared, dressed overall, with a public address system blaring sea shanties which preceded her up the narrow lane, neighbours waving flags and cheering.

Thus with due pomp and ceremony *Cold Feet* left the village.

Now she's in her homeport of Gosport, gently swinging on her mooring, fully rigged, newly painted and almost ready to go. Where to, I wonder? Could it be South America or just round the Isle of Wight – time will tell.

Eve

Family Gathering

On an evening in January 2005, I am dining with friends in the Greyhound. Our table is set with white linen and silver that shines in the candlelight. A young waiter leads in a large group, headed by a diminutive, white-haired, elderly lady dressed in a pale blue cashmere two-piece and silver pumps. They are shown to a huge table at the back of the room covered with a beautiful lace tablecloth, a silver under-cloth peeping through. Coloured helium balloons are attached to the back of each chair, some with 'Happy Birthday' on them. Conversation and laughter add to the party atmosphere.

An elderly gentleman in dark suit, pink shirt, matching tie and pocket-handkerchief rises and asks for everyone's attention. This request does indeed get *everyone's* attention.

'I should like to welcome all gathered here this evening to celebrate my mother's hundredth birthday and to congratulate her on a wonderful life.

'The grandchildren, David, Gillian, Jean and Marcelle and, of course, the babies Sebastian and Nicholas, perhaps do not know their Great Grandmother's story. Lucie, who has come all the way from Singapore with her mother, Swee Hoon, my mother's dearest friend, may not know it either.'

All present gaze at the beautiful Asian women and especially at the mother, perhaps in her eighties, stunning in red and black, who stands up bows and sits down again. The Master of Ceremonies continues:

'My mother, Cecilia, was born in 1905 in the seaside town of North Berwick near Edinburgh, where she lived with her parents and two brothers. They attended the local school and had a happy childhood.

'When she was eighteen, she went to study at Edinburgh Royal Infirmary to become a nurse, not surprising, since her father was a GP. In 1928 she and your Great Grandfather, Alistair Maclean married. Three years later I was born and another three years on my sister, Anne came along.'

The old gentleman acknowledges a lady farther down the table.

'In 1936 we all went by sea to Singapore where my father held a position at the hospital. We lived in a place called Tanglin in a two-storey house with fans in the ceilings, beautiful lawns and masses of help for my mother.

'Unfortunately we were interned for the duration of the war at Changi by the Japanese but we survived the ordeal and returned to Edinburgh where the family resettled. My father took up a position at the Infirmary and we went to school.

'In due course Anne became a teacher and emigrated to Canada. I became a doctor and went to various parts of the Empire before retiring in Bonnie Scotland.

'Please raise your glasses to Cecilia Sarah Maclean who has led a rich and fulfilling life for a hundred years. Happy Birthday!'

Everyone in the entire room raises their glasses and wishes this sweet-faced lady a Very Happy Birthday.

I hope that someone in her family has noted all the things that she's done, where she has been, whom she has met.

In the future many people may live even longer than Cecilia. Every life is interesting and unique and families should record them for future generations.

Elaine

Windsor Soup

Harry, ex-landlord of the Bottle and Glass, resplendent in green beret of the Royal Marines, blazer with ribbons and medals proudly worn, saluted as John and Elizabeth arrived. With a flourish, he indicated where they should park.

Harry's wife, Rene, my mother, Lily, Trevor and myself were watching from the front window; we were delighted to see the surprised and pleased looks on their faces. John unfolded his long frame from the car and solemnly placed upon his head a most elegant, pleated turban, a puggarree, a reminder of his war in India.

Some of the ladies had tried but could not compete with the old soldiers. Rene had a pinny and a cardboard box, with gas mask, my mother had touches of red, white and blue, but no marks for the rest of us.

It was May 8th, 1995, a celebration, fifty years on, of the end of war in Europe.

After champagne, I handed them the menu to awaken their taste buds for the feast to come:

Brown Windsor Soup
Spam Fritters with vegetables if available
Rhubarb and no-egg custard
Mouse-trap cheese with water biscuits
Chicory Coffee.
To be served with Vintage Dandelion and Burdock, 1945.

A drawing of a diving Spitfire added that touch of class.

They were extremely grateful to find that I had deceived them; I can't remember what we ate but I remember the sun was shining, conversation was sparkling, a day I shall remember.

As we made our solemn toasts, to those who had sacrificed their lives, what were our silent memories?

A child's war: woken in the night by a siren screaming; plucked from a warm bed and carried hurriedly to the cold air-raid shelter; the anxious faces, the sudden silences as planes droned overhead; the sound of the all clear. What was a banana?

A woman's war: blackouts, the acrid bomb site which yesterday had been a home; make do and mend, the inability to put a really good meal on the table.

A soldier's war: losing comrades, the stench of killing, letters from home, fear of death, determination to see it through.

Harry, Rene and my mother are dead, all with sad ends for such vital people. Those who are left are ten years older; another twenty years and there will be few alive, even those who were children and babes, who lived through those times. The war museums and cemeteries, the crowds wander through; we want them to appreciate the fears, the hardships and the sacrifices. But how can they? They were not there.

Vera

APRIL
Wired for Sound

Seated in the conservatory, they commented that Eve looked particularly spring-like in a pale lemon T- shirt. Julie admired her earrings.

'They're made from parts of an old piano,' Eve said casually. The others smiled indulgently and shook their heads. Eve!

'Have you ever thought that if we hadn't met at the Creative Writing Class all this wouldn't have happened? We wouldn't have gone to Swanwick, we wouldn't have formed this group,' said Eileen.

'You come to a crossroads,' mused Elaine, 'you take one path, but if you had taken the other...'

Side-tracked

I wanted to dance for as long as I can remember and my first performance, at the tender age of four, was as a water lily. My ballet teacher, Marjorie Middleton, ran the Scottish Ballet School in Edinburgh and was very involved with the Royal Academy of Dancing. When I was a child, Miss Middleton took all the classes and as the school expanded other teachers joined. Years later I took my turn, first to assist and then to teach younger children.

Edinburgh's theatres were always busy and visiting companies would ask for young students to be extras in their productions. So I gave many professional performances, the first being an imp with four others in a play at the Gateway Theatre. Because of our age, we had adults looking after us, were limited in the time we could practise and the money we earned went into a trust.

We had the most beautiful studios, just like the paintings by Degas - large rooms, huge mirrors, exquisite chandeliers and fixed barres. Parents were not allowed to watch and two women ran the dressing rooms meticulously and kept an eye on everyone and everything. Discipline was strict and Miss Middleton went round the room with her stick beating time, or using it to point at a fallen arch, a turned-in toe or knee or to gently lift an arm or leg higher. Accomplished pianists playing grand pianos always provided the music. We had a lot of exams and also took lessons in Tap, Modern, Highland and Spanish, which I liked very much.

I loved this world of make-believe. It was wonderful to dance with performers from the Festival Ballet, Sadlers Wells and Ballet Rambert and be part of their ballets on stage: a child in Nutcracker, a village girl in Coppelia, understudy for Corps de Ballet in Giselle and Swan Lake. Of course there was also the fascination of costuming and make-up. In fact there was no stopping me, as I always seemed to be chosen for principal parts at school plays and musicals. Everyone must have been fed up seeing my name in programmes.

Then my family moved south and, hoping for a scholarship to attend Phyllis Bedell's school in London, I went for an interview in Aylesbury. Felix Aylmer, one of the board members, asked me why I wanted to dance.

'I wish to make everyone happy,' was my naïve reply.

I got the scholarship and an exciting life opened up for me. I was not impressed with the studio of my new school, situated in the basement next to the changing room with a string of indifferent pianists banging away on an old upright piano. My inspiration came from my fellow students. These came from all over the world – Greece, Spain, Israel, Italy, Sweden, Singapore. I especially remember a beautiful South African student who was rushed into hospital to have a tapeworm removed. But the most fascinating was a young lady from Hong Kong, Nancy Kwan, later to have fame in *Suzie Wong* and *Flower Drum Song*. She seemed so confident, yet so vulnerable.

Then I met a dashing young man with blond hair and yellow socks. In due course we fell in love and married. So my life changed completely, but my love of ballet is part of me and for the past forty years I have tried to pass on my knowledge and love of dance and theatre to children wherever we have travelled.

Perhaps after all I just got side-tracked.

Elaine

An Alarming Anniversary

Isabelle took the letter from the bureau, to check again that she had got the right date: January 21. An engineer would be coming to check the burglar alarm. It was a year since she had had it installed, shortly after Michael had died. A year; it seemed like ten years.

She looked out of the kitchen window: eight o'clock and it was still dark; it was sleeting, nearly obliterating the view of the garden, which stretched out before her, a grey, muddy vista, the bushes and trees bending and swaying in the wind. I hate that alarm, she thought. I hate the high, insistent tone when I set it before going to bed and the feeling of panic when I set it before going out, as I grab my bag and rush out in a tizz, in case I don't make it to the door before it goes off. And yet I wouldn't like to be without it, it's like an irritating but watchful neighbour; nosy but protective, allowing me to feel safe alone in the house.

Isabelle wandered from room to room, checking that the engineer would be able to test the boxes at each of the windows. She tidied and rearranged cushions, which were already plump, moved ornaments, and then moved them back. It was a Monday. She hadn't seen anyone since she had shopped on Friday morning. Friends and relatives had been kind to begin with, but she had refused their invitations and now they seldom contacted her. As she gazed from the sitting room window, a fresh wave of despair and self-pity engulfed her. Another squall of wind whipped the sleet against the panes and the day seemed to get even darker.

I hope he isn't like the two engineers who set up the alarm system. They were so young, so quick; I couldn't understand their instructions. They had shouted to each other:

'Indicator armed, Jason?'

'Zone 04 not ready, Max!'

'Alarm instant check ready, Jason?'

'BAT on screen, Max, check battery!'

Isabelle saw a red van drive up and she hurried to the front door. She was relieved to see that the engineer was a mature man, near to her own age. He was about five feet ten, slim, with brown eyes and a kind face. He gave her his security card: Safeguard Security Systems. Alan Fitzpatrick.

'Please come in. What an awful day.'

He smiled at her and, wiping his feet on the mat, looked around. 'Would you show me where the key pad and the control boxes are situated, please?'

She noticed that he was staring at her and a pink flush stained her cheeks. 'Please come this way. The panel is in the hall and the control box is in the airing cupboard, upstairs.'

'My word, you're a real book worm, aren't you?' He surveyed the books which filled shelves and bookcases in the hall, the sitting-room and even the kitchen.

Isabelle smiled. 'We both loved books. Michael was always buying them and so was I, but now...'

'It's my weakness, too, if you can call it a weakness. We can talk about that over a cup of coffee, can't we, when I've finished checking the system?'

'Oh, yes, of course, I'll put the kettle on.' She felt flustered by his suggestion and wondered if she had any ground coffee and hoped the biscuits in the tin weren't stale.

He finished the maintenance tests, which was a relief to Isabelle. She had dropped a cup when the alarm had blared forth; luckily it hadn't broken, it was the blue Italian Spode. She placed a tablecloth on the kitchen table; the coffee was ready in the cafetière, the milk hot in the jug and the chocolate biscuits on the blue and white plate. She sat in the Windsor chair, waiting for him to appear. She felt happy, as though she was having a special friend for a celebratory occasion. She beamed at him as he came into the kitchen.

'My, you are a civilised lady, a cup and saucer, I usually get an old, chipped mug if I'm lucky, and that crockery, why the blue matches your eyes. You must have chosen it for that reason.'

'Oh no, really, I didn't.'

'Well, they're a beautiful blue. Now tell me, are you on the Internet? I noticed a computer in one of the rooms upstairs.'

'No, I don't use the computer very much at the moment. I used to do a lot of work for my husband.'

'You ought to think about it. I've ordered quite a few books over the Internet, you pay with your credit card and they'll be with you the next day. Wonderful, no problem!'

'We used to like going to book shops, especially antique book shops, or places like OXFAM; we were as bad as each other. I haven't been near a bookshop for over a year, I haven't wanted to buy any more books.'

'You must have been in a bad way, hope you'll soon feel like starting again.'

'Starting again?'

'Books, buying books.' Isabelle felt herself flush again.

'Must get on my way. Any problems, give the firm a ring, ask for me and I'll pop round.'

'Thank you. I will.' She watched the van drive away. The rain had stopped and weak rays of sunlight slotted between the branches of an oak tree.

I didn't see those snowdrops before and there are some aconites out. I wonder if the cyclamens are up around the witch hazel? I should rake up leaves this afternoon. But first I'm going to have another cup of coffee and read for a few hours, something light, something romantic - a Maeve Binchy. She propped up the card against the telephone. Perhaps the alarm would play up and he could come back and have another cup of coffee; perhaps she would lend him some books.

Vera

Sister Murphy's Other Path

These shoes are all wrong; they are soft, paper shoes for going
nowhere in
And that's what I'm doing now. Going to nowhere.
And you'll have no need of wearing anything else,
Sister Murphy,
the priest tells me, for it's warm indoors, you'll be now away from
all that harsh weather.
So that is how they will kill me, with their heat and their comfort.
My blood that sings to the cold skies and the grey sea mornings
blown from America.
My blood will slow and thicken with no millrace to quicken it.

And it is because the dog has taken it away, the dog that has always
been there.
Ah now and I shouldn't lay it down to the dog. 'Tis the other way
about.
It is **God**
that has taken it all away, the dog just the messenger.

Leaving the farm to go to the convent, become God's
Sister Murphy.
I fought daily the wart on Sister Ursula's chin, and prayed for
forgiveness.
I fought daily to exorcise my urgent body beneath its habit,
and prayed for chastity. But God was nowhere and I was so lonely.
And cheated. I'd given up so much for Him and He had given me
nothing.

So I left the convent because God had left me.
There was no point to it. And now even after the long times leaving
it is still **Sister** Murphy here on my hollow farm.
But, remembering, I was not a sister to my two men, oh no, far
from it.

Fish Pie and Laughter

They say I wore them out, my two men, with demands of the Soil
and the Bed
but I would be compensated, yes, for the barren years of no
product.
And my crops were abundant and the cows and pigs reproduced out
of cycle
and corn sprang from the stones.
And so it was with me and my five fine boys.
The husbands went away without my noticing it overly because my
boys were with me.

My neighbours spoke jealous sayings of me and how my farm
flourished when theirs were sparse, and snake grass and weevils
invaded
and the dreaded ringrot to the potatoes. They grew suspicion and
fear instead of grain.
Their bad words turned to curses and the soil to dust, my fences
down
and the cattle dying of Twistfoot. But I knew there was no longer a
place for me here
when my last, my baby, my dear one, died in the dark in the night.

On that night of no stars then, it was the dog that was always there,
was there no longer.
Broke its chain in the yard and raced away from here forever.
Savaged the hens it had
protected these years; there was blood and feathers on his fur when
I found him.
Buried him in the field by the sea, next the Child.
Planted sea holly on their graves to shield from the Atlantic winds.
Gave in to the priest of the church that never lets go and went with
them in their van.

Bars on this van stripe the hills as we pass.
The shoes will always be wrong but I will not need them long.
Eileen

Winged Coffin

A wooden coffin, six feet long, twelve inches wide and fifteen inches deep, was strapped onto the roof rack of a car that sped southwards through the Kent countryside.

At the Dover ferry, no one questioned who was in the coffin. The stevedore signalled the car into its parking place and moved on. It could have been granny getting a free ride.

The French Customs men smiled, waved the car on; they found nothing unusual to see a coffin on a car. There could be a stash of diamonds inside, but what did they care? It would mean lots of form filling and sign language. Easier to let it pass.

Weaving through the busy town, then between fields of wheat and maize, the car and coffin diminished into a dot through the avenue of trees.

The Belgians were as nonchalant as the Frenchmen. A nod at the blue passports and onwards, to Liege and Ladies of the Night. What if there had been bags of coke winging by?

A whiz through Luxembourg and then…

Oh! The German border. Now there would be an inquisition. Up went the hand – stop. Another cursory look at Her Majesty's Coat of Arms, a curt nod and off went the car and coffin into Deutschland. It motored beside the Moselle vineyards, alongside the Rhine and over hills that grew into mountains.

The Swiss border had a road barrier and the Customs men spoke English. Now the coffin would be opened. What was that? They only wanted to know if the car had a motorway licence? Of course it did! Find it, someone, and stick it on the windscreen. The barrier was lifted and the car, with brass handles knocking against the coffin ends, passed through. They didn't care if the missing Great Train Robbery loot was inside, more pennies for the bankers.

In the land of mountains, valleys and lakes the journey ended. On a plateau above a village, in a pasture of wild flowers, lay the coffin. The lid was lifted. The mystery revealed.

What were you expecting? A ritual burial?

Sorry, just the holiday playthings – hubby's model glider and the kid's kites!

Where is it now? Hanging from the garage rafters - six feet 'above' the ground.

Julie

The Alternative Path - I'm Stumped

'The Alternative Path' - I'm stumped. It sounds a good subject for BBC4's *Just A Minute*. What can it mean? For example, to reach this file on my computer I went to 'Start', picked 'Documents' from the drop down list and there was my file name. I could have taken a number of other paths – double-clicking 'Documents' on the Desktop and choosing it from there, going into 'Word' and clicking on the folder icon to search for it or double-clicking 'Windows Explorer' to find it there - so many paths leading to the same conclusion.

My grandfather often said, 'Never a door closes but another opens.' That seems to have worked for me. I attended my aunt's girls' school because that was the most economic and advantageous way of my obtaining an education when my parents split up. I did not take 'A' levels because her school wasn't set up for a sixth form. Instead, having a potential for languages, I went as an au pair to Switzerland for a year. To be honest, I don't remember anyone suggesting any alternative paths I might like to choose. On my return, I spent a year at secretarial college, at my aunt's expense. The alternative paths were nursing or teaching, neither of which I fancied, but I did have dreams of becoming a purser on a cruise liner. Some hope there. Instead, I was introduced by the college to The Nature Conservancy in London. Accommodation was found for me in a Catholic hostel, my old bicycle saved me money on public transport and cream crackers and Marmite kept me going from breakfast to supper.

It was only then, being just about independent and going on nineteen, that I discovered alternative paths were available! Other jobs, boyfriends, flats, et cetera – decisions for me to make and stand by.

Fifty years on, I've come to the conclusion that our choice of paths is influenced by those around us – as children, it's by our parents and as parents, it's by our children. My computer has more alternative paths than I have! Sometimes it chooses to crash – perhaps I should do the same.

Eve

MAY
Feet in Mouths

'Vera, you do seem to have a knack of saying the wrong thing. How do you do it?' asked Eileen.

'It's a gift! One of my best was when I was looking down from a double-decker bus at a splendid building, on which there was a plaque commemorating the builder. I remarked to my boy friend: 'That's a very imposing erection,' pointing to the building. The heads of the other passengers whipped round in eager anticipation. Luckily my boyfriend had a good sense of humour, but I wanted to crawl beneath the seat. 'Come on, I can't be the only one. Confess.'

'999' And All That

The morning paper headlines are depressing again!
Flicking through the pages, a short piece headed
'*999 troublemaker put on hold*', warrants a read.

> *A judge gave permission yesterday for 999 operators to ignore a woman who has made 666 calls in a year.*

Can you believe this? A practical joker who thinks the emergency service is for her to play with!

> *Including one because she could not get her video to work?*

Fish Pie and Laughter

She needs locking up and the key thrown away.

> *She has plagued the fire, police and ambulance services*
> *with bogus calls costing thousands of pounds.*

A waster, who doesn't know the value of money. Who is this lunatic?

> *Roberta Roberto, 34, from The Principality.*

My namesake!
What will my neighbours think? Oh, I do hope they read the address, and of course, the age is my saving grace, no one will believe I'm that young.

I'll hide the newspaper, or put it in the dustbin.
On second thoughts, I'll stay indoors this week, dye my hair and wear dark glasses.

Julie

9 9 9
999   999

Why Can't You ...

'Why can't *you* be more like your sister?' was the constant cry from teachers and relations.

I revelled in such praise, but how could Joanne be like me? She was tall and dark, whereas I, a year older, was short and blonde. And wow! Did I take advantage of the situation! Thanks to her, we're friends now but I used to make her life a misery.

On holiday together recently, with time to reminisce, she commented: 'I never understood why Granny smacked both my hands when the pendulum of the grandfather clock was dislodged. I didn't remember doing it.'

'Well, you wouldn't remember something you didn't do. I was the culprit but blamed you,' I confessed fifty years later, 'and as you couldn't remember which hand had done it, she smacked them both.' We laughed, but the injustice had obviously made a deep impression on Joanne.

I wasn't a nice child. Our brother and I got up to all kinds of tricks. One evening, Joanne came in after we'd eaten, to find we'd mixed her cottage pie up with her fresh orange, or what was left of it after we'd shared the quarters between us – one for you, one for me, one for Joanne – and stirred it up. She ate the mess without complaining and never told tales on her two tormenters. Would they have believed her anyway?

We often quarrelled about who should sleep in the top bunk of our shared bedroom. She got there first one night but I turfed her out; she fell to the floor, totally winded, whilst I stood over her, daring her to make a sound.

As teenagers, I stole her boyfriends because I could. One, a young soldier, I pushed in the river; he was annoying. Later, I made sure our holiday in Paris was hell.

I could twist adults round my little finger. Our mother told us, 'Good things come in little parcels'. She was little and so was I. Joanne wasn't.

My sister has had a hard life without my assistance. Left-handed and partially deaf, she had plenty of problems at school. She's been widowed twice and has no children, which is a great sadness to her. Somehow she's risen above it all. She is strong and compassionate, loving, generous and forgiving. Did I help her to learn to cope with adversity and be self-reliant?

The real question is: 'Why can't *I* be more like my sister?'

Eve

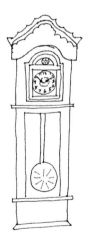

Moments I'd Rather Forget

We all have moments we'd rather forget but in retrospect some are quite amusing. Late for work one day, I slipped my feet into some shoes, and only when I arrived at the office did I realise that I was wearing one black shoe and one blue. Years later in Jeddah, my petticoat fell to my ankles in a crowded mall. Slipping out of it, I gathered it up with one swoop and bundled it into my tote bag. As I was wearing an abaya perhaps nobody noticed?

Attending a school function, also in Jeddah, I got locked in the lavatory and spent a few tense minutes thinking I might have to spend the night there. Fortunately, someone came to unlock the door.

When fake eyelashes were all the rage, I lost one in my soup. On another occasion, I managed to hang onto my wig whilst doing a vigorous dance at the popular nightclub.

I regularly left umbrellas in taxis in Singapore and, when a strap snapped on my sandal in a crowded souk in Libya, a street vendor gave me some string to tie it on.

Holidaymakers got a very different view from the one they expected when walking along the promenade at Lyme Regis. My light summer skirt blew up over my head in a gust of wind and had a will of its own when I tried to pull it down again.

Last year, on holiday in Hungary with friends, we took the ferry across Lake Balaton. Stopping to buy some postcards, to my embarrassment, I missed the boat and had to wait at least half-an-hour for the next ferry to join everyone patiently waiting on the other side.

On a more sober note: a friend told me that his wife had died in childbirth in Madrid due to unexpected complications. Then in Benghazi, an employee's wife was electrocuted when she switched on the Hoover. I am relieved I chose to turn off the electricity when my twin-tub made peculiar noises.

Michael returned from a few days' work in a camp in the Libyan Desert in a state of shock. He had learned that the pilot of the light aircraft sent to pick him up had caught the wing tip on a sand dune and the plane had crashed and burst into flames. This young man had been a good friend of ours.

I was frightened when I was followed into our apartment block in Benghazi by two youths. Heavily pregnant, I climbed the wide staircase as fast as I could, clutching my small daughter's hand. I rang the neighbour's bell again and again, and banged on the door. Just as the footsteps behind me reached the landing, the door opened and I leapt into the hallway, pulling my daughter with me. My neighbour, Iptisem, admonished the youths in loud Arabic and slammed the door in their faces.

I used to have an old-fashioned passport with two others attached to it at the back, sealed by the British Embassy, as the stamps in all three were necessary. It was comforting although cumbersome. Now I have a new one, a little maroon sliver that gets lost in the bottom of my handbag. When I go through immigration my heart pounds in case I've mislaid it.

I expect there will be more moments I would rather forget but perhaps life would be less interesting.

Elaine

Bad Trip

Muscat in the Sultanate of Oman was my favourite sales visit in the Gulf. Kuwait had no booze, Bahrain did, but the humidity made my hair flat, and Qatar had no pavements. Dubai was sophisticated with well-ordered traffic, and its policemen wore the tightest of lovely blue-grey jodhpurs. But Muscat, at the very tip of the Gulf was beautiful, and when the plane wings dipped down between the mountains at sunset, my heart always rose.

I had a love-hate relationship with our agents there, which is common amongst most British sales companies. They always assumed that agents did nothing to promote their wonderful products, and that they themselves could do it far better.

My company manufactured Arabic-English diaries and could emboss, for example, a gold cement sack on the cover to present the perfect give-away, year after year after year; it really was a lovely scam. But my favourite logo to date was a perfectly formed sprung mattress for the Kuwait Mattress Company.

Muscat Office Supplies at least boasted a real Sales Manager, who rattled me about in his un-airconditioned car to unlikely customers in far out industrial areas. This trip was to be no different.

'You must not be late, Mrs Ileene, because today we visit a Very Important Man at Oman Cement Works. I have tried and now succeeded for this appointment for many weeks and you will be happy with this.'

'That is good indeed, Mr Prakash, and does he have a need for diaries for his company?'

'I am sure that he will definitely have a need and you will explain all that you can do for him and so on...'

Mr Prakash had a touching faith in my sales ability.

'I will collect you at five thirty tomorrow morning from your hotel.'

Oh Joy.

The sun rose steadily as we drove towards Rusayl Industrial Area thirty kilometres out into the desert. Normally I would have revelled in the journey, but the unmistakable smell of Mr Prakash's polyester trousers, gently warming in the heat, pervaded the small car. Mr Prakash also had a salacious interest in the lives of the minor Royals and, since I lived in Royal Berkshire, assumed I must be in the know.

'All that toe-sucking and stuff,' he started without preamble. 'That must have been terrible for your poor Queen.'

His understanding of some English idioms, as well as the fact that his information was largely gathered from out-of-date magazines in Smart Man Barbers on Hilal Street, didn't help the conversation.

The meeting with the Advertising Manager was not a success. He did not know who Mr Prakash was and could not recall his ever making an appointment.

However, with the usual perfect Omani hospitality he ordered us coffee and talked a little about Chelsea Football Club and the world trade price of cement. We did not stay long since I knew nothing of either subject. He never had, nor ever would give our diaries away to his customers.

'They're a little passé, don't you agree?' he asked, brushing a speck of dust from his immaculate long white dish-dasha. 'I'm giving away these little jobs next year. Rather fun aren't they?' He produced an electronic digital diary which probably made tea as well. I admired it for three seconds, thanked him for his time and left.

'Well, I think that went quite well, Mrs Ileene. We'll be in there next year now we've broken the ice.' He really believed it.

So I was not heart-broken to find on my next trip that Muscat Office Supplies had appointed a new Sales Manager. Ram Mirza was smart, young and extremely keen. He was a qualified doctor from Bombay, but could not get a medical job in Oman. I felt foolish and inadequate teaching him about sales inserts and print runs, when he knew what went on inside my body and I did not. But this did not lessen his enthusiasm and he saw nothing incongruous in the situation. We spent a concentrated week together, and I left feeling that at last our diary sales (and therefore my commission) were in safe hands. He was also a much better driver than Mr Prakash!

Returning in September with my export manager, James Griffin, we were met at Seeb Airport by the Office Supplies car. A smart young driver leapt forward to meet us and I thrust the first of my bags into his outstretched hand. He looked a little surprised and opened his mouth to say something.

'Sheraton, please,' I told him quickly to forestall any unnecessary conversation. He nodded, staggering under the weight of my suitcase and sample bag. I never travelled light.

'Your guy must really have shaken things up,' remarked James. 'Last time I came through they'd forgotten I was coming, much less met me at the airport.'

'You're not as pretty as me,' I said smugly.

'But I earn more, Miss Smarty-Pants, *and* I can sack you.'

We both laughed as the driver finished loading our bags into the boot.

As the car sped down the Seeb Highway I leaned forward to the driver. Perhaps I'd been a little abrupt in my manner at the airport and I wouldn't wish to offend him.

'Tell me, is the Sales Manager who was a doctor still with the company?'

Silence.

'Oh yes, Madam, it is me. I am still here, and I am happy to serve you in every capacity that you require.'

There was not, nor ever will be, anything to say.

In the back seat my boss looked at me and drew his finger softly across his throat in a silent slitting motion.

Eileen

A Learning Experience

Karen pushed open the staff room door, both arms wrapped around a stack of exercise books that reached up to her pointed chin. The room was heaving: teachers consuming coffee, making coffee or queuing up to make it, regaling each other with horror stories. The windows were steamed up and children were milling in the quadrangle, their shrill tones filtering through the glass and adding to the cacophony. She sank into a seat next to Phillip.

'Thanks for getting me a cup. I need it.'

'What happened? Class play you up?'

'No, they were lambs, but I had to get ready for my next lesson, the dreaded 10C.' Phillip looked concerned. 'Don't worry, I'll win. It's hard teaching boys after an all girls' school, but most of them are OK; it's Ziggy and his cronies, they're little devils.'

'Fancy going for a drink tonight?' Karen smiled and nodded eagerly. 'See you at dinner-time. Keep on punching!'

I wish I was six feet tall, with a firm jaw and piercing blue eyes, Karen thought, as she watched Phillip leave the room, instead of a five foot midget, with big boobs, no shoulders and three-inch heels.

The class was lined up outside the laboratory, a mass of heaving, shrieking bodies.

'Quiet, please. No one comes in until you've stopped talking.'

They moved to their usual places. I made a mistake letting them choose their own groups, she thought, as she watched Ziggy's gang occupy the back two benches. She placed the register, class books, board marker and her Parker pen on the teacher's desk and the lesson started.

After twenty minutes, the tension in her shoulders eased; the movement of the pupils was purposeful, the noise level acceptable. She moved to the back of the class. As she bent over a microscope she heard:

'You don't get many of those to the pound. What a pair.' She whirled round, pulling the edges of her lab coat together. Ziggy was grinning at her, his eyes creased in amusement; he snorted with laughter.

'Go and stand by my desk. Face the wall. I'll deal with you in a minute.' The smile was replaced by a sullen look and as he shuffled to the front, his mates jeered at him. Later, he made a surly apology and returned to his bench, to more jeers from his companions.

Karen moved to the front of the class; she was pleased, the lesson was going well. Oops, haven't done the register. She looked for her pen, the gold Parker pen her parents had given her to celebrate her first teaching job. It wasn't there. Ziggy. He'd stolen it. Horrid, lecherous boy.

'Class, please put everything down and pay attention.' She waited until all their puzzled faces were looking at her. 'Someone has taken a pen from my desk; a gold pen, inscribed with my name. Perhaps someone has hidden it for a joke. I will give that person three minutes to bring it to me. While we are waiting, finish your notes.' There was whispering amongst the pupils and she could hear Ziggy's mates asking him if he had taken it; he kept shaking his head and darting looks of hate towards her.

The three minutes were up.

'I will give the person who has taken the pen, one last chance. I will leave the room for two minutes. If the pen is not on my desk when I return, all the class will be punished and no one will leave the lab until it is found.' She glared at them and swept from the room, the noise rising as she left.

She tried to hear what was being said. She could hear Ziggy's voice above the others. She looked at her watch and po-faced walked back in. The pen had not been returned.

'This is disgraceful. Ziggy, come here and bring your bag with you.'

'Get lost. I didn't take your stupid, crappy pen. I'm not a thief.' He spat out the words and clutched his bag to his chest.

'Come here at once.' He remained in his seat, glaring at her. The tension in the room was electric.

'Amanda, take this note to the Headmaster.' The class gasped.

A resentful silence hung over the laboratory as the bell rang out and they could hear children making their way to dinner. As their cries died away, the sound of purposeful footsteps was heard, becoming louder as they approached the laboratory. A collective groan emanated from the pupils.

Mr. Ralph Owen exploded into the room, Karen's note in his hand. 'Sigmund Karelius, come here,' he boomed in a strong Welsh voice.

Ziggy slouched towards the front of the class.

'Stand up straight, boy. Now answer me truthfully, did you take Miss Adam's pen?'

Ziggy straightened his shoulders. 'No, sir, I'm not a thief.'

Mr. Owen stared at Ziggy for several seconds. 'I believe you. I haven't known you steal before. Are you prepared to empty your bag and have your pockets searched, to prove your words?'

'Yes, sir.'

No pen was found.

Ziggy was sent back to his seat

Mr Owen whispered to Karen. 'Look now, Miss Adams, I don't think the pupils know anything about the pen.' Karen felt wretched. 'We'll try this, if it doesn't work, I'll search every pupil in the room.' He turned to the class, 'You will search in your bags, on the floor, in the cupboards, to try and find the pen. Miss Adams and I will do the same. Five minutes - silence please.' Bags were tipped up, cupboard doors banged, pockets were turned out.

'Search your bag again, Miss Adams, let the children see that there is fair play.' He moved towards the teacher's desk, pulled out the partly-open drawer and froze. 'Miss Adams!' He pointed into the drawer. There was the pen. Mr. Owen gave her a withering look. 'I'm sure you will know how to deal with this situation.' He swept out of the room, closing the door behind him.

Karen raised her eyes to the class. They stared back at her in silence.

'The pen is in the desk. It must have rolled into the drawer at the beginning of the lesson.' She paused. 'I would like to apologise to all of you, especially Ziggy. I accused you of being a thief. I'm sorry, Ziggy, I hope that you will be able to forgive me.'

Ziggy grinned at her, 'Fair dos, Miss, I was rude to you, you lost your rag; my Mum does it all the time.' Giggles from the class. 'I accept your apology, no hard feelings. Can I be excused homework this week?'

'Thank you, Ziggy, you're a gentleman. All of you, I'm sorry I've shortened your dinner-time. Ziggy's idea was brilliant: no homework for everyone this week. Class dismissed. Take care, have a good weekend.'

Mr. Owen glided away from the laboratory door. He could hear the children calling out: 'Bye, Miss, have a nice weekend.' They sounded happy and relieved.

He smiled. She'll do, he thought.

Vera

JUNE
The Fish Pie Club

They stood in front of the menu board, ready to place their orders before commandeering the conservatory. At last, thought Vera, five orders for fish pie! 'I knew you'd all come round to it in the end,' she proclaimed triumphantly.
So the alternative name for the group was born.

It was nearly four o'clock when the girl from the bar presented them with the bill and gently told them that the pub would be locked up in a few minutes.

As usual the craic and stories had been engrossing, time had flown. They agreed that there was no substitute for good conversation.

Erotic Sandwiches

We found the Red Onion Saloon busy at lunchtime and the bartender, working alone, looked frenzied. Where had all these people come from? There were no cruise ships in the bay today. As we sat down, the bartender took a deep breath.

'Hi everyone,' he called. 'I'm on my own to-day – but relax – I'll be with you as soon as I can.' There was some grumbling and a few chairs scraped back as people departed the lofty wooden building. We stayed. We were in no hurry and were weary from our shopping and sightseeing. From the list of sandwiches, Jackie chose a Harlot, James, a Strumpet and I, a Trollop - 'Real turkey breast served with American cheese on sourdough bread'. Such was the fare on offer in Skagway's most exclusive bordello, but this was 2001 not 1898. By all accounts that was the time to have been here – at the height of the Klondike Gold Rush.

Whilst our Bartender rushed from his small sandwich-making pantry to his bar serving his customers he kept up a running commentary. 'We've been here since 1898, then liquor was served down here and women like Popcorn Lil, the Oregon Mare and Pea Hull Annie were kept busy in ten little rooms up there.' He pointed to the ceiling. 'Others were,' he hesitated, 'the Belle of Skagway, Klondike Kate, Big Dessie … What was your order, sir? Three beers coming up.' He patted a shelf behind the bar. 'There were ten dolls here. When a girl had a customer, her doll was laid on its back and as soon as she was free, the doll was sat up again. Waiting prospectors then knew she was ready, willing and able,' he said with a grin. 'Here's your Painted Lady, madam.' He placed a curried halibut salad before the customer, 'and a coffee, the sugar's on the table.'

'How did the bartender know when she was free?' cried one young man.

'Er,' he considered, while hurriedly putting together a Ménage-à-Trois sandwich. 'Well, it was like this – each cubicle was connected through a copper tube in the floor to the cash register down here. When he heard the rattle of gold coming down the tube, he knew she'd been paid, and up went her doll.' At this point the bartender's girl friend arrived and, seeing how busy he was, stayed to help.

'What did it cost?' called another customer.

'What did what cost?' he asked puzzled. 'Oh, yes, five dollars. The girls preferred it in gold and they also hid gold nuggets and private tips under the floor boards.'

By this time, we had received our refreshments and were tucking into our erotic sandwiches.

'When are you opening the upstairs again?' queried a fat elderly gentleman. The bartender grinned and winked but said nothing. I thought he'd probably like to say 'Not in your lifetime, Sir!'

Later he told us that when the railroad came to Skagway some buildings were moved closer to the depot. The Red Onion was moved in 1914, by one horse, from Sixth and State Street to Broadway. 'Problem was,' he continued, 'the Onion was dragged round the corner backwards and ended up back to front. They had to saw off the front and back walls and switch them round.' Was he having us on?

Our patience had been well rewarded. Those who'd left had missed good food and great entertainment - a romp through an historic brothel - American style.

Eve

Trust Me, I'm Not a Guide

'Hallo, welcome to Islamic Cairo. Did you want to see Mohammed Ali Mosque – The Citadel? I am so very sorry but it is closed for prayers and renovation for three hours but do not worry, I can take you to see another much better mosque which is not closed and it is on my way home ... And that bad taxi man has left you at the back end to the entrance which is a very long way from here and anyway, it is closed, yes.' *Hesitation.* 'No, no, I am not a guide, please do not think that. I am a Law Student at Cairo University in my Third Year and it would be my very great pleasure to take you there and introduce you to the real Islamic Cairo.'

Brown eyes yearn in an honest face. *Why are we so suspicious, why suspect someone so proud to show his country's heritage of architecture and religion? And besides, he is a law student, not a guide. He has said so. And how lucky that he was waiting here, just where our taxi had dropped us.*

'I have friends in Wales and Barking and other places in England. Do you know Barking?'

No we don't know Barking but are impressed that he does.

We proceed at a fast gait down through narrow streets where donkeys sag under lopsided loads and the small shops have dark insides. A seven-year old boy beats the hell out of a rusty Lambretta part. The entire contents of the world's Lambrettas are being recycled in a parking lot behind him.

'I am married with two children. We marry young in Egypt. When I am qualified I will work for the good of my country and help its people.'

'Gosh,' said William, impressed. 'Don't you find it hard studying with young children about?' He had found it bad enough in a student hall in Southampton with all the necessary distractions of bars and girls.

'Oh no, it will be good.'

Another man joins us as an outrider sheepdog so that we don't get away. 'Welcome to Islamic Cairo.'

Our growing apprehension must be obvious.

'It is all right. He is my friend.'

Friend? They do not even speak.

'This is a very good mosque we go to, oh the very best.'

We arrive, and are told to take off our shoes, but is there a surrender fee? We are still mistrustful. But no, we are allowed to keep them and carry them in our hands.

We enter the mosque. It is beautiful with engraved ceilings where birds and branches swish aloft. A fountain plays in the centre of the courtyard. We are bidden to sit on the carpet and listen to the story of Mohammed. John sits on a white plastic chair because his knees hurt.

'It's very kind of you to bring us to this beautiful place but surely we intrude upon your time?' John ventures.

There is a cough, and an elderly cleric steps out from a hole in the side wall. He is irreproachably old and holy. 'To see all the mosque and help towards its holy upkeep there is a very small charge which I am sure you will not mind.'

Do we? Better not, and for me there is delight in entering a previously forbidden place.

'How much?'

The hard sell.

'Forty Egyptian Pounds'

This is the equivalent of twice the taxi fare and a few beers on top, but like little lambs, we go.

'See, the money should be placed by you in this strong locked box and the key will always be kept by me.' More steadfast brown eyes and we do meekly as he says.

We climb up the narrow minaret steps, and reach the first level, looking out over an unprepossessing landscape. I am reminded of my rooftop washing lines back in Kuwait; but this is a desolate scene with scratching chickens and scrawny goats below.

'This was caused by the Earthquake in 1992,' the man who is not a guide says.

'How terrible it must have been,' I murmur. 'And you were here in Cairo then?'

'Ah no, I then was in Alexandria,' he replies. *This fortunate man is always in the right place, be it taxi-drop or earthquake.* 'You can see very near the wonderful establishment of Dr Karim who has the finest School of Papyrus in Cairo.' *True colours now.* 'There are some terrible cheats who write on banana leaves. Would you believe this? *I really don't care. Yellow cigarette paper would do as long as we can get off this horrible roof. It starts to rain.*

'You would learn greatly from a visit there and could purchase...'

'No.'

The showman at last senses defeat. 'Perhaps a little gift for my children at Christmas time?'

As we emerge from the stairs and leave the mosque, we imagine that we hear a scraping noise, perhaps of a rusty key unlocking a box? But we close our ears as we do not wish to hear.

Eileen

The Art of Conversation

Margaret surveyed the knickers arranged in islands on the shop floor: high-legged thongs, tangas, strings, minimalist nudies. Goodness, where were the low-legged coveralls? Slowly she circled the islands. Was the world full of women with tiny bottoms and no cellulite? She found some hip-slip shapers, which promised to reduce your waist and thighs immediately you squeezed into them. What would George think if he saw her in these? Margaret imagined his face turning purple, his mouth opening and closing, like a silent movie actor. But would he say what he thought? No, he never did. If only he would 'communicate'. Like that man on *Vanessa*, he told his wife he was a transvestite; if only George would reveal his secrets.

She heard a voice, strident, full of anxiety. A young woman was talking into her mobile phone. She was tall, slim, all in black. She circled the knickers, in her own bubble of sound, umbilically connected across the ether to her communicant. Margaret, fascinated, edged closer.

'I've just bought the most fabulous dress in all the world, it's fucking fantastic.'

Oh, fancy using the F word about a dress, it must be good. Wish I could see it. I wonder who she's talking to, can't be her mother?

'I've got some sexy shoes to go with it, I can't wait to show them to you.'

Oh, Margaret thought, creeping nearer, is she going to buy her underwear now? Will it be a tanga with a balcony bra?

The young woman became agitated. 'Darling, you have forgiven me? I'm sorry for what I said this morning.' She stomped around the sports bras and headed for the nighties. Margaret shuffled after her.

'I didn't mean to hit you when I threw the Robbie Williams CD.'

Pause.

'Yes, I *know* I was discus champion of Surrey, 1999.'

Pause.

'It was only a little CD; if it had been an old, plastic job, I'd have taken your head off.'

Margaret shivered with delight. Oh, what power.

'I didn't mean to wipe out all your football statistics, my hand slipped.'

Pause.

'I'm sorry I cancelled Sky Sports, put it down to pre-menstrual tension.' Still talking, the woman headed for the escalator.

Margaret reluctantly decided that she couldn't follow. How wonderful to be able to talk immediately to someone you loved, to tell them how you felt, what you'd bought.

'George, it's me, are you there?' There was the noise of cardboard and plastic being ripped, and Margaret emerged from the kitchen into the sitting room, hands behind her back.

'I've bought you a present, and one for me as well.' George lowered the newspaper. With an air of triumph she thrust two mobile phones under his nose. *The Daily Telegraph* started to tremble.

'I'll call you when I'm shopping, I'll be able to tell you what I've bought, where I am, when I'm catching the bus. I'll be able to call you at the golf club, ask you what you'd like for dinner. Won't it be lovely?'

George's face had turned an unattractive shade of puce. Spluttering and stumbling he pushed past her. She followed him through the house, and from the kitchen window saw him speed across the lawn and into his shed.

Oh, thought Margaret, it's been too exciting for him. Pity he didn't take his mobile, I could have rung him up and we could have had a chat about it.

Vera

'Hello George …Margaret here. Over …'

Bus Talk

As the number 22 bus pulls up outside Marks and Spencer in the King's Road, a multitude of people spill onto the pavement mixing with an even greater multitude of bodies trying to clamber aboard. Although at the front of the queue, I appear to be about to be left behind when, yes, 'Three more,' shouts the conductor putting his arm behind me to bar anyone else getting onto the platform.

I find myself on the top deck sitting next to a young man listening to his Walkman: feet tapping, fingers clicking, oblivious to his surroundings. Opposite, another young man tries to balance an enormous board on his knees, which keeps slipping and falling onto the woman in front of him, who glowers at him – 'Sorry, so sorry,' he says and then, as the bus swerves, the board falls across onto yours truly! Why did I end up here? Well! At least I am on my way home.

The owner of the Walkman rises to his feet. I assume he wishes to get off, so I stumble to my feet clutching my packages and yes, the youth with the board is getting off too. He would have been quicker walking, the pace the bus has been going. Relieved, I move across to the window seat and am joined almost immediately by an attractive, trendy twenty-something with endless jean-clad legs, equally long eyelashes (they can't be real) and manicured nails painted blue with gold tips. I look out of the window.

'Did you get what *you* wanted?' a voice enquires. 'I have so many bargains. I can't believe it.'

I turn round, the young woman is beaming at me!

'Oh yes, thank you. I got most of the things on my list but didn't have much time, so wasn't really tempted. Perhaps another day. There seems to be lots of lovely things in the sales for young people like yourself.'

Pulling open a large cardboard bag, my young companion pulls out a short white coat followed by a matching frock. Out of a plastic bag comes a pair of boots with pointed toes and what look like five inch heels, then from another, a sequinned evening bag with matching minuscule top and from the last a profusion of tiny under-garments of different hues.

'What do you think? I got them all for a song.'

'Well! You must be pleased you've got so many bargains.'

'Yes, I suppose so,' she says, the lower lip trembling, 'but I don't need them, and next week the shops will have their new stock and I will see more things, buy more things.'

'Why do you buy things that you don't need?' I ask.

'I'm bored really. Every month I get my allowance and I just spend it. Lulu, my sister got married and has gone to live in Barcelona. I miss her so much.'

'I think you must go and visit your sister. And why not do some course here in London?' I suggest, conscious that I sound very motherly and down to earth.

'What a good idea, Oh, it's my stop! Thank you. Bye.' And off she goes down the stairs, off the bus and into the dark that has fallen on our London Town.

Elaine

Talking Numbers

The instructions say 'If you want help, phone...'

'Good morning, this is Dye Hard Hair Consultants.
If you want to enquire about our fabulous hair colours, please press 1.
If you want to know about our stockists, press 2.
If you want to know about our full range of products, press 3.
If you want to know how to order a product, press 4.
If you want to speak to a consultant, please press hash and wait.'

The sweet tones of music fill my ears, *Over the sea to Skye...*
I hum along with the tune, this is pleasant, then, 'Sorry to keep you waiting,' brings me out of my musing.
This has cost me four minutes so far.
Back with, *Over the sea to Skye...*

The window could do with a clean; I could write my name in the dust.
Hey, a van has pulled up across the street at number 51. They're having a new kitchen delivered. Good job I'm sitting here, I would have missed seeing it going in.
'Sorry to keep you waiting,' pipes in an accented lilt.
Six minutes!

A repeat of *Over the sea to Skye...* I'm beginning to hate this lyrical drone.
The new postman looks harassed in the rain; he's just dropped all the envelopes on the wet pavement.
Eight minutes!

A real voice, 'Marie here, Customer Services, how may I help you?'
'Hello, I bought a box of your blonde hair dye...'
'Sorry to butt in, but you need to redial and press option 5. Thank you for calling.'
'But there is no opt...'
She's gone, the stupid girl has gone!

Press redial.

'Good morning, this is Dye Hard Hair Consultants.
If you want to enquire about our fabulous hair colours, please press 1.
...press 2.
...press 3.
...press 4.
If you want to speak to a consultant, please press hash and wait.'

Ten minutes!
And I'm back to square one.
I shout at the handset: 'You must be joking.'

Two can play at putting the receiver down.
I'm not going through all that again. I'll keep my white Granny locks. I'll get a refund. That'll knock their profit down.

Julie

JULY
The End of a Journey

The vine was in full leaf, creating a restful shade over the table at which the five women sat.

'A toast,' said Julie, 'To us, the Swanwick Babes-'

'I prefer the Fish Pie Club,' interrupted Vera.

Julie ignored this remark and continued: 'To a year of friendship and laughter.'

'Not to mention all the hard work, you slave driver,' said Eve.

'It's been a journey, I've learnt so much,' said Elaine.

'Ah, journeys, that reminds me,' said Eileen and began her story.

In Touch with the Real Thing!

I had read about Prison Ships in history but had not, until we came to Delhi Main Station, seen Prison Trains. But there one stood on Platform Three with faces peering out hopelessly from between bars on smeary windows for a last glimpse of loved ones. I shivered and thought how fortunate I was not to be among them.

'Do hurry up, darling, we'll never get out of Delhi at this rate.' My husband had promised to take me 'somewhere special' as a reward for twenty-five years of sock-washing and his ranting at the radio, on a journey we would never forget.

I did not feel particularly special as I heaved my rucksack onto a shoulder (more used to swinging a Gucci bag), and staggered under the weight. He didn't notice. He was too busy haranguing anyone in uniform who looked as though they might know something.

We had only been in India for three days and already I was a subservient wife. Actually I quite liked it. It was a change. In Real Life I ran my own business, got myself around airports, sorted visas, hotels and dealt with the occasional letch. Now I just waited.

It was December 1992, the year of the Ayodhya Mosque riots, and random curfews were in place throughout India. Delhi was cold and I wanted to go anywhere that was further south. Udaipur, at over a full day and night's journey seemed to be the best option and not yet under curfew. It was also a long way from Delhi with its smog and street beggars.

'Sorted,' he said, and strode off in a direction I was intended to follow. I stumbled after him. But he was getting on the Prison Train! He was a Quaker and although prison reform was of great importance to them this was ridiculous. And *he* had warned *me* about being late! I stood waiting for him to alight. But he didn't. Instead his furious face loomed through a grimy window. 'Are you coming or are you going to...' His outburst was drowned by a blast of noise and smoke from the train. This then was the *opulent* First Class, Three Tier Sleeper we'd queued for in Delhi Station two days earlier.

He intended me to get on this thing and because I couldn't think of anything else to do, I obeyed.

Admittedly, it didn't look quite so bad once we were inside, and I didn't notice the bars too much because we were taken up with the Interlopers. They sprawled across our First Class seats, and hawked and spat particularly vile streams of ineradicable betel juice over our future bedroom floor. Nutshells crunched under foot. A violent-looking man with bright red hair got out his chatty-tin and started to eat a bright red curry. It smelt delicious, but the globs that dropped on the floor would probably not do so in the sleeping hours. We felt that we should protest but he gestured to us to share his meal by waving a chapati at us, so we couldn't. They'll get off soon we thought. They didn't get off.

We were nowhere near Udaipur, but they were still with us. And they had happily settled into a game of cards. The train rattled on. Milk churns were thrown down a random embankment. We shifted our sticking bodies on the hot rexine seats. It grew dark; hours passed and the Betel Juices played relentlessly on. They had finished their curry picnic and were now on to small and filthy-smelling little cigarettes.

Three hours later the train slowed to avoid wandering cows on the line. The BJ Gang as one collected cards, tins, and bundles and disappeared down the embankment into darkness.. We watched them go with relief. I wondered if they knew where they were?

'Oh, sure they do,' said my husband. 'They'll have an Auntie out there in the dark cooking them fresh chapatis.' His voice was tinged with envy. His aunties were more of the ham salad and tinned peaches variety.

Then followed the worst night of my life. Thin, mean blankets made from unhappy sheep had been reluctantly prised from a guard who hadn't heard of our Special Sort of Ticket. The cold seeped through my bones and the string bunk became an icy tomb. The train stopped at made-up places where no one got off; it shunted, scraped, took on coal and was a creature of itself. Worse still, my well-regulated body was telling me that it had needs. I was on the top bunk in the dark, and the unspeakable hole that passed for a toilet, was way down a corridor of sleeping bodies.

I felt a spasm of pure and total hatred for my husband.

'You can stay in these faceless hotels any time,' he had said, when arranging the trip. 'We'll be far more in touch with the real thing doing it this way.' I hadn't really been listening, painting my toenails and trying to watch Morse.

I had not the will on my return to scale up to the Tomb again, but stood in the corridor and prayed for dawn.

I could phone our solicitor and institute divorce proceedings from Udaipur

Pink streaks appeared across the sky and the air felt warmer. We had stopped at a small station and a man was selling tea in small clay cups from a huge urn on wheels. I stretched out of the window and bought one. The tea, sugar and milk were all boiled up together and it was delicious, warm and sweet. Along the length of the train, arms were reaching out through the thinning mist and rupees were thrown down on to the platform.

In FirstClassThreeTierSleeperland, the Husband was still asleep and snoring lightly. I allowed myself a moment of smugness. 'Ho, shame you missed the beautiful sunrise as we passed through Chagripur,' I could imagine myself saying at some later well-chosen date.

As the sky gradually lightened, shapes of mountains and forts appeared in the distance. The lumps and bundles strewn along the corridor began to stir. Was it possible that we were there yet?

'Bloody awful night, didn't sleep a wink,' he said. 'See you were well away the noise you were making!'

I decide to take both the house and the car in the divorce settlement.

Eileen

On Guard

1.30pm
The wooden chair was placed in the centre of the room. There was a slight moulding for the posterior and a slatted back to hang the shoulder blades on.

1.35pm
Maud Jenkins sat down.

She shifted her weight. It was a chair designed to be uncomfortable, to keep the sitter awake. Her eyes looked at the clock, watching the minutes tick by.

Behind her, Charles grunted, snorted down his nose, and he moved his head from side to side in the winged chair. His feet were propped on a footstool. He looked really comfortable.

Opposite Charles, Beatrice and George sat together asleep on the paisley sofa. She whistled like a branch-line steam train and he overtook her with his main line rattle. They were like the rain and shine weather people that hung in the hall.

1.45pm
The clock chimed.

1.50pm
Maud stretched her legs and arched her back. It was only fair she took her turn, but she was bored and that made her eyelids droop. As she slipped sideways the corner of the chair back dug into her spine. There was no chance of having forty winks on this!

Primrose fidgeted in her sleep, sighing every few seconds. Her thin claw-like hands plucked at her skirt. Did that mean a good or bad dream?

Maud took another look at the clock.

The overture of snores was like an orchestra tuning up, minor and major notes not in harmony.

1.55pm
Maud reached over to the portable radio and pressed the button.

Eighty decibels blasted out. The snoring stopped. Heads came up. Bodies straightened. Hands moved to take the cups of cold tea.

2.00pm
Two vibrating chimes sounded.

Hearing aids were adjusted, eyes focused on the set and the theme tune of *The Archers* rang out.

Maud rose and went to sit in her comfortable chair. It would be another fortnight before she was on guard duty again.

Julie

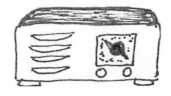

To Port Sudan

James had agreed to go to Port Sudan in November, on condition I'd be there for Christmas – an unusual concession. Normally employees had to spend three months on an overseas contract before wives could join them.

So here I am on this cold, squally Tuesday, 22nd December 1959, at London Airport waiting to board the plane. Our belongings have been stored in my in-law's loft – as recent newlyweds we don't have much. I've left my job, scoured London for clothes suitable for temperatures of 100°F+ - not easy at this time of year, said my goodbyes and am looking forward to the adventure. I'll see James to-morrow.

The journey as far as Rome is uneventful except that we land at 20.30hrs, forty minutes late, due to head winds. Refreshments are served in the transit lounge, then dinner. There's a problem with the plane. We take our seats again soon after 22.00hrs, taxi down the runway and back to the apron. We're given the option of staying on board or returning to the lounge. I stay put. The wrong choice. It's hot, airless, noisy, uncomfortable and the babies on board are whining.

At 02.00hrs we're told we'll stay the rest of the night. We stagger through passport control and on to a coach. It's after 04.00hrs by the time hotel rooms are allocated and five hours later Italians are screaming up and down the corridors to wake us up. There's some hope we'll be able to leave at 13.30; that's changed to 14.30, then 15.30.

In the meantime, we're taken on a sightseeing tour of Rome. If only I weren't so tired, this could be really interesting, but I do note they're getting on with construction work for the Olympic Games and recognise some of the sites I've seen in photographs.

We eventually leave at 17.00hrs on Wednesday, 23rd December and are due into Khartoum about midnight. I'm not sure what I do then but am too tired to care. The plane is unbearably hot and most of the lights have been switched off. Will I get to Port Sudan by Christmas?

Khartoum airport looks somewhat worse for wear at 01.00hrs on Thursday, 24th December, as, I'm sure, I do. There's duty of six pounds to pay on my camera; the officer accepts Sterling but doesn't recognise a five-pound note. Unexpectedly, the Company Secretary John and Jill, his wife, meet me. As I climb into their car outside the airport, I have a vague impression of grey concrete pillars pitted with bullet holes. The cotton-stuffed mattress at John's home is hard but it's good to lie down for a few hours.

This is the first and last time I meet these kind people. My brief visit to Khartoum lasts six and a half hours. I am in the air again and on my way to Port Sudan by 07.30hrs that Thursday.

As our small aircraft comes into land, the steward walks down the aisle with his flit-gun spraying us with some unpleasant insect killer, then the door opens and the moist heat belches in. I gasp as I walk down the steps and across the sand-covered tarmac. How can anyone live in this temperature?

I'm exactly twenty-four hours late.

To-morrow is Christmas Day – will I be allowed to sleep?

Eve

132

Lily's Last Journey

'Forty-five minutes late, due at 12.45,' the woman in the green coat declares; we had taken turns guarding the suitcases and visiting the station monitor. The rain falls relentlessly. A charismatic man starts to organise a passenger protest group and a railway official hands out complaint forms. I am hungry, thirsty, sad and nervous. In my suitcase, enclosed in a mahogany casket, are the ashes of my mother, Lily McDowell. We are making our last journey together, 'up North', to bury her in my father's grave.

A small, tinny Virgin train pulls up; first class consists of one small capsule at the front. I haul the case up the steps and look around; there are only nine seats, they are all taken and I can see that the rest of the train is full.

'Excuse me, I think you are sitting in my seat.' An unattractive man, about forty, with long, greasy hair, looks up at me. No reply. He wears a leather jacket and has removed his trainers. 'You're sitting in the seat I've booked.' I wave the reservation ticket in front of his eyes.

'The guard said I could sit here.'

'May I see your ticket?' He grudgingly produces it. 'I see you have not booked a seat. Look at the slip on the back of this seat: Reading to Runcorn. This is my seat. Are you going to move?'

'The guard put me here. I'm not moving unless the guard finds me another seat.' The other passengers look away in embarrassment.

I turn and ask the girl in charge of a drinks-trolley, to summon the guard. A young man offers me his seat, but I am reluctant to accept and let the lout off.

'Thank you, but only until the guard arrives.'

The lout wriggles uncomfortably. 'I've got a bad back, I can't move too well.'

'And I, young man, am very old.' The swine doesn't even dispute this fact!

The guard rolls into the compartment, red, flustered, clutching his mobile phone. 'Madam, have you a problem?'

I return the seat to the polite, young man.

The guard listens. 'I'll try and find you a seat somewhere else in the train, Madam.' Poor Brummagem guard, voice quavering, sweat trickling down his face.

'I booked this seat. I shall stand here until this man gives it to me.'

At last, holding his back and moaning, he rises.

'You can have my seat, I don't mind moving,' the nice young man says to him. The vile creature accepts with a grunt. Unfortunately, his new seat is directly opposite me. The guard sighs gratefully and is immediately assailed by other passengers.

'Sorry about that, but the guard did put me in your seat.'

I look at him contemptuously and curl my lip. I decide he must be an ageing rock-person. I stow the case in a space across the gangway, beneath the seat of a young woman and her attractive daughter. The mother is talking to the guard; they will miss their connection to Holyhead and the ferry to Ireland.

The compartment is small and most of the lights don't work. The girl with the trolley starts her journey down the train. As a first class passenger I am entitled to a free drink. The guard returns and writes on my ticket that I can claim a refund. Fantastic!

The disgusting specimen puts on his filthy trainers as we approach Birmingham. He has made several calls on his mobile, talking about gigs - I was right. As the train pulls into the station, he rises and pulls a leather rucksack onto his back.

'I see you have made a full recovery, a Virgin miracle, no doubt!' He gives me the evil eye and the other passengers snigger.

I relax now that the fiend with the sweaty feet has departed. The polite young man returns to his seat. I close my eyes, lulled by the rhythm of the train.

'Lily, Lily!' a voice cries. Fear grips me. 'Lily, Lily, come here.' Who is calling my mother?

I open my eyes, sit up and look for the case. It's still there. The young woman is holding out her arms to her daughter, who is running up the aisle. 'Lily, come to Mummy, at once.' She is enfolded in her mother's arms, and plonked on the seat.

There are two Lilys in the carriage, one on the seat and one underneath it. I flop backwards, my nerves shattered. I should have used Securicor.

Vera

Are We There Yet?

Zambia 1973

In the early hours of the morning we set off in a Government vehicle with an African driver – our destination Mongu, three hundred miles west of Lusaka. It was a long journey on a dusty track, mile upon mile of almost arid plain with nothing of interest. Suddenly, five hundred yards ahead, we saw a huge petrol tanker stationary on the road. Running towards us at speed were two young Africans, arms and legs moving like pistons. Our driver stopped and we all looked in the direction the young men pointed. Two huge elephant were a few yards off the track near the tanker, ears flapping, feet stamping, trumpeting loudly. We spilled out of the car, the driver, Michael, our two young children and myself. Our son took a few steps forward and waved, our daughter joined him and we all stood – a little group in the middle of this vast landscape looking at these mammoth beasts.

A few minutes passed, we took photos, and suddenly the elephant turned round raising clouds of dust and ambled off. We got back into our vehicle and followed the tanker along the track. Our driver, in his early fifties, told us that he had never seen such large elephant and perhaps they thought the tanker was an adversary but, seeing the children, they decided to leave.

The rest of the journey was sticky, uncomfortable and uneventful but not once did the children ask, 'Are we there yet?'

Mongu, bustling capital of Western Province, stands on high ground overlooking the Zambezi Flood Plain. It is the kingdom of the Lotse tribe and famous for the Kuomboka Boat Ceremony. This takes place in May when Litunga, the king, goes down the river from his Wet Palace to his Dry Palace.

We pulled up outside the building Michael was looking for and, whilst he was inside, I took the children into the public lavatories. We shot out again quickly - they were filthy. A pretty young girl with a baby on her back beckoned to me and took us a few yards away behind some trees and showed us a rondaval. Inside it was cool and dry with a deep hole in the ground. We came out happily into the fading afternoon light, the blonde, blue eyed sun-kissed children attracting much attention.

We spent the night at a Travel Lodge, not far from Mongu. With our legs covered in aluminium foil against the mosquitoes, we sat outside watching the beautiful sunset. In the distance thousands of flamingos rose from the marshes.

Next day we visited the local school and met a teacher sent out from America with the United Nations for the summer break. I was concerned as she was very young and her pupils were men with an average age of twenty-six. I was asked to read from Romeo and Juliet but they were more impressed when our daughter read in her clear schoolgirl English.

The children loved the mosquito nets in the bedrooms. After a second night in the Travel Lodge, Michael completed the task of connecting a radio link between Mongu and Lusaka and we set off on our return journey. We took a longer route so that the driver could visit his family and we could see his clean, tidy village. Everyone was very friendly and we took more photos. We saw kudu, even a few giraffe but no elephant and as we drove into Lusaka, the lights of the city twinkled in the dark.

But not one little voice had asked, 'Are we there yet?'

Elaine

 THE END